THE SHEPHERD LORD

GEORGE PETER ALGAR

Published by

MELROSE
BOOKS
An Imprint of Melrose Press Limited
St Thomas Place, Ely
Cambridgeshire
CB7 4GG, UK
www.melrosebooks.com

FIRST EDITION

Copyright © George Peter Algar 2009

Reprinted 2010

The Author asserts his moral right to
be identified as the author of this work

Cover designed by Catherine McIntyre

ISBN 978 1 906561 96 3

FSC
www.fsc.org
MIX
Paper from
responsible sources
FSC® C013604

Printed and bound in Great Britain by:
CPI Antony Rowe. Chippenham, Wiltshire

ACKNOWLEDGEMENTS

THE WRITING OF THIS BOOK WAS MADE a lot easier by the support, tolerance and encouragement from friends and family. A special mention goes to Luke, who is my biggest critic and most enthusiastic supporter. Not to mention the ghostly spectre or whatever it was that pulled me out of bed before the waking hours nearly every day to pen this story.

Part of the proceeds of the book will go to the Towton Battlefield Society.

Front cover incorporates image by Graham Turner from Towton 1461 (Campaign 120) by Christopher Gravett © Osprey Publishing Ltd.

FOREWORD

THE WARS OF THE ROSES, AS WE call them now, produced the biggest ever pitched conflicts on English soil, and feuds that lasted generations, none more so than those of the Lancastrian Cliffords, whose name is resonant in Shakespeare's Henry VI and earned John Clifford, the ninth Earl, the nickname, 'Blackface' or Butcher Clifford.

After John's death at the Battle of Towton, for fear of reprisals, his son and heir, Henry, was spirited away under the care of a shepherd whose wife had wet-nursed the boy.

So great was the fear of a Yorkist backlash that he was raised in deprived circumstances and remained illiterate until he was restored to his family estates after Richard III was killed at Bosworth.

This novel is concerned with the period that lay between these great and well recorded events; the period between John's death in 1461 and Henry's succession to his titles after 1485, two decades of mystery as far as Henry's life is concerned. Local legend has him raised in secrecy by a shepherd, so that his existence would be concealed from the Crown.

In the novel, this shepherd is brought to life in the character of Tom Lawkland, who becomes Henry's surrogate father. Tom, a wise and quick-witted man, narrates his own parts of the story – and those of Henry – in his own characteristic voice.

Little is known about the man who put his life at risk to raise the 'Shepherd Lord', as he was known, just as little is said of Joseph who brought up the infant Jesus. But think what stories these characters have to tell. What did they witness when great affairs of state and life-changing events were going on around them? What traits of character did they nurture in their charges?

These mortal men are the unsung heroes.

What captures the imagination is the contrast between the life of a simple shepherd and that of one of the ruling families of the North of England. Wordsworth eulogised it in his poem, *Song at the Feast of Brougham Castle,* and it is said that Emily Bronte based the character Hareton, in her novel, *Wuthering Heights*, on that of young Henry, deprived of his birthright.

There is allusion to the tale in a poem, *The Nut-Brown Maid,* that was very nearly lost, but discovered and revived, by Samuel Pepys. Other than that, the story has not been in mainstream literature for generations.

The story is too powerful to be forgotten though.

The shepherd, looking after his flock, has long been a symbolic and evocative image. It is held in the three main faiths of Christianity, Judaism and Islam. This book is the untold story of how the not-so-simple shepherd looks after his ward and teaches the boy qualities of dignity, hard work, inner calm and an appreciation of God's bounty. He is raised as one of nature's gentlemen, qualities that hold him in good stead when he is propelled back into the power house of Henry VII's England.

I came across the story by accident, when researching some family history. According to family legend, it was a commonly held belief that John Clifford led a reluctant Bolling family to the battle at Towton where he lost his life and they their lands, as a consequence of supporting the Lancastrian cause. The more I researched the matter, the more interesting facts emerged. The Wars of the Roses were not wars between the two counties of Yorkshire and Lancashire, as is commonly thought, but wars between cousins arguing about who had the right to rule England. Large parts of Yorkshire were under the Duchy of Lancaster and were loyal to the Lancastrian cause. The advancing Yorkist army, mustered mainly from the South and Cheshire, must have seemed a threat to those living on Yorkshire soil. In fact it was not until the accession of Richard III, another character much maligned by Shakespeare, that the people of the North warmed to the Yorkist cause. But all of this is as nothing when compared to the desperate plight of a young mother, trying to protect her child from the forces of evil and having to give up the thing she holds most precious to the care of others.

A story of epic, biblical drama and one that is a true part of our heritage.

CONTENTS

PROLOGUE

THIS IS THE TALE OF TWO MEN, Henry, tenth Lord of Skipton Castle, and Moses Lawkland, a lowly shepherd. Yet, they are both one and the same man. The first, sired by John 'Blackface' Clifford, scourge of the House of York; the second raised by me as a simple shepherd lad who tended his flock without a care in the world.

How so? War. For the sake of land-hungry men who fought their own kith and kin to gain more riches than a man can spend in a lifetime. Men who would kill a young innocent child.

Yet when all is said and done, when the last sword has been sheathed, when the rain washes away the last drop of blood, when the ravens have picked the rotting carcasses clean, when the treaties have been signed and these land-hungry lords granted new estates, war changes nothing much at all. The land will heal itself, the seasons will turn and ordinary folk will find a way of returning to their quiet, worthy, wholesome lives. If those who sit on their thrones and count their riches knew this, happen they wouldn't be so eager to wage their bloody feuds and disturb the workings that keep the world turning round and put food on a man's table.

If we were to trade places, perhaps there wouldn't be so many grieving widows and mothers. Happen? But I know nowt of what my lords refer to as 'political matters', nor have I any desire. For them that knows seem to have nowt but strife and doubt in their life. Them that doze fitfully in their mighty palaces don't get a trouble-free night's sleep like we that spend our nights underneath the stars. I know that now, I learnt it from a young lad who knows both worlds, and if you were to ask him straight, he would tell you that power and wealth won't bring folk half as much happiness as can be had on a hill, watching the stars at night on taking in the first breath of a new morning. I am happy with my lot, and in this war-torn kingdom, this makes me the most privileged of men. Stories like mine are easily forgotten through the years and so the real lessons in life are lost with them. But the land knows the lessons, the hills and the sky have always known, and I listen and find peace.

Chapter 1

Skipton Castle - Tom Lawkland

THE WALLS OF SKIPTON CASTLE HAVE NEVER been breached[1]. That is a fact. The walls are a full thirteen feet thick and sat on bedrock so they can't be mined.

My Lord, John Clifford that is, took great delight in showing me the defences and telling me how he'd butcher anyone that were daft enough to try attack us.

For a start, tha' can see for miles around from the watch tower and there's a sheer cliff and a river, Eller beck, protecting the rear. To approach tha'd have to come up a steep bank and then tha'd have to get through the thick castle walls. Supposing tha' did, and tha'd got through the gatehouse. Why, the portcullis would drop and trap thee in, and soldiers would cover thee in boiling oil and burning pitch and drop gurt big boulders on thy head.

Supposing tha' got past that and tried to cross to the castle. Why, it's a killing field. Tha'd get shot up the backside from archers on castle walls and down tha' throat from cross-bowmen, what are manning the keep. And supposing tha' got over the moat and broke down the doors to the old Norman Tower. When tha' got in there, another portcullis would shut thee in and floor would give way and tha'd land in a pit. Once tha' fell down there, tha'd be a sitting target. It would be a charnel house.

It has to be that way an' all, for there was a castle here afore the Cliffords came, that was breached right enough. That was hundreds of years ago but folk still talk about it now. David, King of Scotland, sent the Picts and part of his Scottish army down to Craven to spoil and pillage.

In this work o' destruction, no age or rank, nor either sex were spared. The stout wooden keep was put to the torch and bairns were butchered in

---

1. Even the mighty Oliver Cromwell with his heavy artillery could not take Skipton Castle from Anne Clifford in the English Civil War.

front of their parents, husbands in sight of their wives, virgins and matrons of condition were carried off wi' other plunder and stripped naked and bound together with ropes and thongs, goaded for'ards wi' the point of sword and lance. Scotch bastards. Barbarians. The lot of 'em.

That were never allowed to happen again. The Cliffords built a castle out of stone this time, wi' high towers and stout walls. Come and try it on now, if you dare!

So, no one's ever made a dent on walls even. Not even tried. But I were there the day that Skipton Castle were abandoned. Some things you remember as clear as yesterday.

It was early morning. The guards shivered in their armour, standing on the battlements, stamping their feet and clapping their arms to the sides of their jakes[2] to get circulation going.

"Don't you feel the cold?" asked the captain, steam coming from his breath.

"This isn't cold," I grinned at him. "You should spend a winter on those fells tending the sheep and then tha'd feel the bite o' the north wind."

I was waiting for an audience with her ladyship, a new experience for me. Due to the bad weather I thought I'd better report to her on state o' lambing. I had a reputation of losing very few but I knew she'd be worried nonetheless, for sheep are the staple source of income for our estate.

My Lord, John Clifford, was away to war. He trusted my judgement and would let me handle the shepherds without anyone else's bidding, but I promised to keep account with Her Ladyship to put her mind at rest. I had My Lord's trust. I was named Tom, in honour of his father, Thomas, the eighth Lord Clifford, him as commanded the field for the Lancastrians at St Albans and was slain by York. I served the family well, there was no doubting that. That's why I was Reeve over all the other shepherds.

"What's that?" I said, as my eyes caught a flicker on the horizon.

"Can't see a thing," replied the captain, straining to focus on the distance. "Can you see anything, Walt? Your eyes are a sight younger than mine."

"Bugger all," grumbled Walt from the depths of his sallet.[3]

"No, there," I insisted. "Follow that path near that top sheep fold; a rider,

---

2. Armour, typically steel plate on leather.

3. Helmet, commonly worn in the Fifteenth Century.

and he's moving fast."

"Well, I'll be dammed. All that counting sheep on the fells must be good for your eyesight," said the Captain. "I can just see him; he's coming into view now. He'll have news of the war. I hope he's bringing a Yorkie's head home on a pole. I'll put the bugger up over the keep."

A great war horse clattered on the cobbles as it sped through the gate. It was flecked with great froths of sweat and its flanks were bloody with the goading of spurs.

"That's the arms of the Bollings, but I don't recognize the rider," said the Captain.

"It's young Tristram," exclaimed my Lady Margaret, walking up behind us, summoned by all the commotion.

Margaret had more than sheep to worry about. Two small boys to care for and her husband was away to war, as I've said. He was the driving force behind the Lancastrian army. His fatha may have been killed by the Yorkies at St Albans but he'd got his own back twice-fold, killing the Duke of York and his brother at Wakefield. He'd got a right reputation and he wasn't about to stop now. Every man from the age of fifteen to fifty was called to arms and he'd made a right old scene, charging around the county with his riders, calling the farmers from their fields and the huntsmen from the forest. If there was any fighting to be done, he'd be in the thick of it. Lady Margaret knew that.

I didn't know her that well then but I've got to know her a lot more over the years. My wife was her handmaid for a while, even wet-nursed her bairns. She reckoned there was none like her but I'm me own man and like to make up me own mind on folk. Give 'em a summering and a wintering afore you decide, as we say here in Yorkshire.

She was a bonny young thing, right enough. A beautiful face framed by dark hair, very thick, and so long that it reached down to her calves. She was kind enough but had that reserved air that some of the nobles do. Didn't feel she should show any emotions or fear to the likes of me, but I could tell she was fretting. Fretting for her husband. Fretting for the future of her boys and, in fairness, fretting for her servants and the common folk. Lord John always looked after his own and made sure that everyone on his estates were well treated and well fed. Tha' can't have a well kept estate if tha' workers are ill-fed and not up to much. So, he cared for us. That's why so many rallied to his cause, right willingly. He was our Protector and we owed him our duty, in return. But back to the events of the day.

The horse skidded to a halt, its sides heaving with exertion. The rider all but fell out of the saddle, removed his sallet and knelt in front of Lady Margaret with his head bowed.

After what seemed like an age he raised his young head and her distraught face searched his for news.

He was a handsome young man, no more than sixteen summers, but his face told of horrors that no man should see. Without him saying a word, my Lady knew that Lord John was dead and she turned, ashen, bringing her hand to her mouth.

"My Lady, my Lady," he rasped through ragged breath. "All is lost. Your husband, my Lord John, fell in the field. The Yorkists have routed us. I am sorry, so sorry, to be the bearer of such news. They will be here soon. My father, Robert, bid me ride here without delay to warn you."

"You have done well, Tristram, arise and take some refreshment," was her calm but distant reply. There was an awful silence as she took stock of what had happened and what she must do. She had to control her trembling and think clearly. She was the sort that had been schooled to keep her head in a crisis. She took a deep breath. She was more reposed now. Grieving for her husband was put to one side as the safety of her lads was now foremost in her mind.

I bowed and said, "My Lady, Lord John has made provision for your sons …" but she silenced me with a look.

"How fares your father? Is he safe?" enquired Lady Margaret of Tristram.

"He sped fast to Bolling Hall, My Lady, to put our affairs in good order and hide our treasures. We will be lucky to escape with our heads, if not our lands. Edward did not take prisoners and he's thirsty for revenge."

"Your father was ever a wise man. Follow his prudence and you will be safe. First give me news of the battle and then return to him with all speed."

"The battle; there was never such a battle, My Lady. 'Ere it started, I rode with Lord John and the Flower of Craven[4] in a skirmish, the like that we had trained long and hard to do.

"You know what My Lord was like. Full of daring and a deep-rooted hatred for those who killed his father and would take our lands. He led an attack on Ferrybridge on the eve prior to the battle and took Fitzwalter by surprise. He hit him with force so fast and so hard that Edward thought all the Lancastrian army was with him. Many a Yorkist drowned in the river and Fitzwalter was slain. All the might of Edward could not shift My Lord from that bridge. He sent his champion, proud Warwick, to attack us but he was too slow for my Lord Clifford and we sent them running with our jeers ringing in their ears. I fired my bow at Warwick when I saw his standard illuminated by the burning tents and I'm sure the arrow went home true, wounding him in the leg. He wheeled his horse and ran with his tail tucked under his legs back to his master. Lord John said I would be commended to Queen Margaret for that.

But crafty Edward sent his men upstream at Castleford and gave chase. We made good to escape but just as we reached Dintingdale, but two and a half miles from Towton, thinking we were safe we slowed our pace and it was at that place there was an ambuscade. John Neville and I were the only men to escape the field. Lord Clifford and my comrades in the Flower of Craven paid dearly with their lives.

"Our outriders knew what was happening but I'm ashamed to say that Somerset would not come to our rescue. They would not risk their forces in open field. Better they had shown Lord John's courage and he still might live."

My Lord, dead? The news stunned me. It was only a matter of days ago that he was here with his riders, raising the militia. I knew what we must do now. We must get the lads away from the vengeful House of York at all costs. They would not want a Clifford heir to plague them and My Lord had entrusted me with his plans in the event of his death. Lady Margaret looked to be taking it all very calmly while my heart was pounding and my thoughts were racing.

Tristram continued, "The eve of the battle was the coldest night for many a year but at least our men had fire and shelter. Many of the Yorkists slept out

---

4. John Clifford's crack troops were known as the Flower of Craven. Hard fighting, hard riding men.

5

in the open and it was a wonder they survived the night.

"We had the greater numbers and Percy had a detachment of cavalry conceal themselves in Castle Hill Wood, near Towton, my father and I amongst them. Our ruse was to take them by surprise and turn their left flank during the heat of battle the next day.

"On the morn, there was a great blizzard and the snow stung the eyes of our archers so that they could not see but two paces out into the distance. Wily old Lord Fauconberg tried a ruse de guerre[5] from the French Wars and had the Yorkist archers advance forty yards under cover of snow and then loose their arrows at our men, knowing that the prevailing wind would give them the advantage of range. They then fell back.

"A captain of the archers later told me that our reply fell well short but under such provocation and being snow-blinded, we fired back at will. Somerset was livid at this indiscipline but his hand was forced. He had no option but to advance our billmen.

"Our men fought bravely, especially the conscripted men. They were fighting for their own soil and slaked the frozen ground with Yorkist blood. We were gaining ground.

"At the sound of the trumpet, our cavalry charged from the cover of the woods. We smashed into their flank," Tristram said, with a fist into the open palm of his hand, his eyes blazing, "and never have you seen such fear in the eyes of men, for we wanted revenge for my Lord John and our North Country dead. They started to turn. One by one they started to turn and we advanced over the bodies of their dead, but then Edward, seeing what was about to happen, charged across and urged his troops on. He dismounted and stood shoulder to shoulder with his men. Well, I say shoulder to shoulder, but he stood a good head taller than any man on that ground. He laid about him with a great broad sword and his men, seeing that they were in the presence of their future King, rallied and made good their column formation.

"Our horses would not charge the column and all we could do was watch from our steeds while our pikemen engaged the battle line again.

"We fought all that day and the field was littered with dead. Slowly, but slowly, our men pushed them up the hill. Once over that knoll, my father said,

---

5. Trick of war. Lord Fauconberg campaigned in the Hundred Years War with France and was one of the leading Yorkist Commanders.

they would turn, make no mistake. Even that haughty Edward would not hold them but, just as the day was so nearly ours, Norfolk arrived with new troops to support their right flank.

"The battle lines turned. Lord Dacre was killed the same way as your husband, with an arrow in his gorge," he recounted. At this My Lady winced.

"The noble Percy was injured and gaps showed in our ranks. Some men turned tail, first one and then another. We pressed hard on our flank but it was to no avail for on the other there was now a rout and desperate men ran down the hill into Cock Beck. It was swollen from a little brook into a mighty flood plain and many drowned, weighted down in the freezing water by their armour. The day was lost." This was said with a heavy sigh.

"Those that survived were chased in the direction of Tadcaster, but my father, knowing the lie of the land, helped make good our escape. We were lucky to have sturdy mounts for many of those on foot were hunted down and slaughtered where they stood. That is all, My Lady, and now you must make plans to leave this place. If I can be of any service, my sword arm is yours, as it was your husband's."

Lady Margaret smiled at this earnest young man and said, "You honour me by your pledge of loyalty and courage, but I have made preparations for this moment and will away to my father's house. I will be safe there."

"But the boys?" pleaded Tristram, stopping mid-sentence, not wanting to make plain what fate awaited them at the hands of the House of York.

"Fear not," said Margaret, "for a lioness looks after her cubs as well as the mighty lion. I will conceal them from the murderous jackals that follow. They will be in safe hands until they grow to be as strong as their father and take revenge on those who would deprive them of what is theirs by birth."

At this, Tristram made for his horse, drew his poniard and cut a pendant from the harness, giving it to My Lady. She looked at it for some time, smiled and then commented, "It's beautiful. Storm martens, the arms of the Bollings. I have never seen such exquisite work."

The young man, colour now returning to his cheeks, explained, "It was made in Limoges for my great-grandsire many years ago. The enamel is the best in the world but the art of making it has been lost since the Black Prince sacked the town and killed all those that lived there. I give it to you as a token.

If you, or your sons, ever need help, send this to me and I'll come to your side as fast as my mount will take me."

My Lady smiled. "It is good to see that chivalry is not dead. You put yourself in great danger by declaring yourself my knight in shining armour."

At this young Tristram blushed.

"But now is not the time for gallantry. Now is the time for stealth and concealment. We must bide our time but our time will come. Like the Virgin hiding her child from Herod, I will take care of mine but they'll not meet the fate of our Lord on the cross. They will live on and see these usurpers spewing their blood in the gutters.

"You have done well, Tristram. Stay alive. This token of your loyalty will be of no use if your head is severed on the executioner's block. You are young and I can see you are lusty and headstrong. Take counsel from your father and restrain from rash actions. It may take many a year but you must wait until the time is right to strike back. Rest assured I will call for you at that time," and at that she clasped the pendant to her lips, kissed it and placed it safely in the purse on her belt.

The young fellow stood there, his chest swollen with pride and a tear in his eye. He leapt on to his horse, tugged at the reins, turning it a complete arc, and waved as the great beast skittered across the cobbles. He looked every inch the soldier but I could not help feel great sorrow for what awaited him and his father. Things were about to take a turn for the worse for all of us in the North.

CHAPTER 2

THE FLIGHT

Give her wings that she may fly,
Or she sees her infant die!
Swords that are with slaughter wild
Hunt the Mother and the Child.
Who will take them from the light?
--Yonder is a man in sight--

Wordsworth

THE FIGURES TOOK ON A BIBLICAL HUE as Tom Lawkland led Lady Margaret and her two small sons on the pack animals. He strode out grimly in front with his stomping shepherd's crook, looking neither this way nor that but eyes firmly focused on the distant horizon.

The landscape was monochrome in the weak winter sunlight with vast pewter skies and scudding grey clouds.

Townsfolk watched on, without passing comment, as if they were watching a funeral procession and indeed, in a way they were, as they were watching their old lives walk away into the distance. They were helpless to stop it. The Clifford family was in exile and they would have new masters now that their beloved Lord Clifford and his brave riders from Craven were slain on the battlefield.

"Where are we going?" asked young Henry Clifford. "Why are we leaving the castle without my father's soldiers?"

His mother smiled thinly. "We are going on a journey to see your old nurse, Bessy, good Master Lawkland's wife. You do remember her, don't you? She has children of your own age that you will be staying with. It will be

9

a great adventure and you'll live out in the countryside in the lovely Yorkshire Wolds and have lots of friends to play with. Won't that be exciting?"

"Why can't we stay here? When's my father coming back?" pleaded Henry, whilst his brother, oblivious to all this, pretended to be an archer shooting at the scattering sheep as if they were a mighty army.

"I'll explain all when we get there. We've had quite enough excitement for one day and I want you to be good boys for Master Lawkland," explained Margaret. "He is a very clever and kind man and you are to do as he bids. Your father left very strict instructions."

Margaret was holding back the tears when she said this and Henry, being a sensitive boy, could sense that something was amiss, and held back his questioning and contemplated the scene in front of him. He knew Tom Lawkland well, as one of the important men in his father's estates. A huge, raw-boned, grim figure whose face would break into a broad smile when his father made some jest or other about the weather, the price of wool or the rustic shepherds he managed. He was gruff and spoke in the vernacular but, as his mother said, was a kind and caring man. He would bring orphan lambs for the boys to feed and wonderful soft sheepskins for their beds. He felt safe in his presence. It was a link to his father's world of tall, towering, rough-spoken men. Strong men who indulged small boys like him with mock fights, men who would wink and tell him how brave and strong he would grow up to be.

His mother was suffering. That he could tell and Tom was quiet, even for him. Seldom had the young lad ventured so far from the castle and he took all in as they continued on their journey.

Tom Lawkland said goodbye to every living and inanimate thing as he helped them on their flight. Goodbye to the beautiful limestone country, landscaped by the sheep for thousands of years. Goodbye to the crouching homesteads in the valley. Goodbye to the tough Dalesbred sheep. Goodbye to the racing Eller Beck stream and the curlew in the air. Even the sky would not feel the same where he was going and he knew that he would not return for years to come. This was the land where he was born and he grieved at having to break his deep bond with it.

He was to be father to Henry, whilst his brother, Clifford's younger lad, Richard, was sent abroad. He was to raise Henry as his own son. Train him how to be a shepherd and how to talk the way of the country folk. To blend him into the countryside so those that followed and sought him would not know him as the noble Clifford's rightful heir.

The journey was a grim one and all he could do to take solace was to repeat a verse of the twenty-third Psalm over and over again.

Yea, though I walk in death's dark vale,
Yet will I fear no ill:
For thou art with me, and thy rod
And staff me comfort still.

He half expected the dark lowering clouds to open and reveal guardian angels, with trumpets to herald them on their journey, but then, he realized, he was on his own. He was the one who was chosen for this task and would have to bear the mighty burden. How was he to cope? This was new territory for him but there was no use bleating like a newborn lamb. He'd a job to do and there was only one way to do that and that was as well as he could. Make no mistake.

Lady Margaret and her father would be nearby at Londesborough, whilst he'd be given a farm, but any contact with Henry would have to be kept to a minimum. Even among the loyal retainers on that estate it would not do to arouse any suspicion. These were desperate times.

CHAPTER 3

EDWARD

Edward, Head of the House of York and self-proclaimed King of England, was in a foul humour. His retinue were near to tremulous in his company.

"Bring me the muster rolls now!" he demanded. "I don't want to delay a minute in rounding up these treacherous bastards. Every last man of them. Anyone that's not dead on the battlefield has skulked off back home and are no doubt plotting the next rebellion."

"Here you are, Sire," said a worried scribe, scuttling across the chamber.

Edward snatched them from his hand and tapped his poniard as he surveyed the list.

"I want it seeing to that everyone on this list is attainted. I want a visit from my marshals to evict them from their pox-ridden estates and have them thrown out on the highway with the beggars. Every bloody Percy, Dacre, Tempest out there, right down to chicken-shit families like the Bollings. What is it that makes these cursed northern counties foment with trouble? It has been the same since the time of the Conqueror. We have polluted our noble blood by marrying them off to too many local wenches. That's one thing the Conqueror got wrong but, like old William, I will harry the north until every last rebel is brought to book. No one is to be spared my displeasure.

"And as for the Cliffords, the bloody butcher Cliffords," this said with his face crimson with rage, "I want their devil spawn offspring bringing to me."

"Tread softly my brother," soothed Richard, Duke of Gloucester. "Do not react in the heat of the moment. I have suffered as much as you at the hand of Blackface Clifford, but we need to give this our most careful consideration. Infanticide would outrage the populace and we do not want another rebellion on our hands."

"We did not make mention of harming the young rascals," was the sardonic response.

"We merely want to look after their welfare and ensure that they are brought up where our benevolence can be used to greater effect. Have Eldroth brought to me. He has a nose as good as any hound's."

At that a liveried page, wearing the quartered surcoat of England and France, left the chamber with a bow to do Edward's bidding. Already, proud Edward had taken on the trappings of a king, even though he was not yet anointed.

Richard, sensing the rage storming in his brother's breast, tried a more conciliatory approach. "You have won a great battle, my brother. The biggest and bloodiest battle fought on English soil.[6] Probably greater than any battle fought in Christendom.

"My liege will not need any reminder from me that after such a great battle, when peace has been declared there is need for a strong leader. A strong leader that is just and noble-minded and treats all his subjects with the same fairness of hand. Many of these people here had no choice but to fight for Henry. The peasantry were conscripted by these Northern earls. The minor nobility had even less choice. They are ..."

"You need not remind me of the laws of Kingship and fealty," interrupted Edward, now standing and towering over his younger brother. For the onlooker, it was interesting to note how different they looked, though from the same branch of the tree. Edward was exceptionally tall, with blond, shoulder-length hair and a look that would brook no contradiction. Richard was tall by normal standards, though not nearly as tall as his brother, and darkly handsome with piercing blue eyes. Though different in nature and looks, there was a strong bond of brotherhood between them that no man could divide.

Edward continued, "I don't give a fig for what obligations they had elsewhere. England has a new ruler now. England is for the English, not these mongrel bastards and their mercenaries. Why would they choose to support such a weak leader as Henry? I'll tell you why, so they can exploit and manipulate him to their own advantage.

"They're in it for land and gold. Why, even the cack-handed Kerrs came

---

6. The Battle of Towton was the biggest battle fought on English soil. It is said that up to 28,000 men died that day – more fatalities than any of the WW1 Battles on the Somme.

down from Scotland to join in this battle, intent on plunder and rape before they scuttle back to their shit-hole in Scotland. Now, their dead will fertilize our kingdom's soil. Where's that scribe?"

At that, the scribe stepped to the fore, his double chin pulsating like a frog's and his bulging eyes fearful of this firebrand King. Edward commenced his list of attainder, the scribe scribbling away with his quill furiously.

"And where also Henry Duke of Somerset, Henry Percy, late Earl of Northumberland," Edward dictated, reading out a long list of Lancastrian supporters. He was in full flow when the summonsed Eldroth entered, bowing lowly and taking in all those about him with his shifty eyes. Edward waved for him to wait by the brazier and continued with his list of those to be attainted – which literally accused them of being of 'bad blood' and forfeiting them of land and titles.

He concluded with, "in the said shire of York, called Saxonfield and Towtonfield, accompanied with Frenchmen and Scots, the King's enemies, falsely and traitorously against their faith and liegance[7], there reared war against the same King Edward."

Edward smiled. Revenge was a sweet dish, he thought to himself. A good king had to be ruthless and he was no exception.

"Eldroth," he purred, "bring your cut-throat carcass over here and listen attentively to what I am about to tell you."

Eldroth was a thin-faced, black-avized[8], evil-looking fellow, who could not quite keep still in the presence of such mighty nobles, and squirmed like a weasel. He was a veteran of the French wars and had been kept on as a retainer to the House of York to do any dirty work they might have.

"Now Eldroth, as I understand it, you were born round these parts and understand the wretched language of these folk?"

"Yes, Sire," replied Eldroth with a ferret-like smile, exposing his yellowing teeth. My father was a cooper in Halifax and my mother ..."

"Enough!" snapped Edward. "I'm not interested in your poxy father and the whore that gave birth to you. You are to accompany Sir Thomas Courtenay here as he travels round this shire with his list of attainder. You are to make discreet enquiries about the whereabouts of the Clifford whelps. When

---

7. Taken from the original document of attainder.
8. Old fashioned word for black-faced i.e. evil looking.

I say discreet, I mean discreet. I don't want you spooking them into hiding. Is that understood?"

"Yes, Sire," responded Eldroth, shifting his weight from one foot to the other. He looked slyly at those around him in the room, although he dare not meet Edward's eye, and almost giggled with relish at his new task.

He minded Edward of a weasel, dancing before a startled rabbit, and he instinctively knew that he had picked the right man for the job. If anyone could find Clifford's sons it was this man.

Eldroth bowed again and departed with the saturnine Sir Thomas Courtenay, looking a most unlikely pairing. Richard, Duke of Gloucester, shuddered when he left the room.

"Feeling the cold, brother?" enquired Edward.

Chapter 4

Brough Castle,
East Riding of Yorkshire

Now that she was in the relative safety of her father's home, the normally resolute Margaret Clifford sobbed uncontrollably in his arms. She had lost her husband to a horrible death at Dintingdale, shot through the throat whilst he removed his gorget[9] to slake his thirst. She felt a deep guilt that she had not even had time to contemplate this sudden and brutal departure of their life together. Theirs had been an arranged marriage, as most were in those days, but she soon fell for the bold, daring, handsome man that was John Clifford. She could hardly begin to imagine what his last thoughts were as he choked on his own blood. Thoughts of his home, his wife, the safety of his children and sheer bloody anger at those who had taken his life. She wept openly.

And now, she must say goodbye to her boys. John had made sound plans as to what they should do in the event of his death but she never thought she would have to invoke them. She knew it was for the best. She knew they would be safer out of her custody but, nonetheless, what mother would not break down with such sorrow if they were faced with the same dilemma?

Her father, Sir Henry, sensing her thoughts, soothed her as he had done when she was a child, stroking her hair.

"Fear not, my daughter," he said in a calm, reassuring voice. "Your husband has thought this through very well and even speaks to us beyond the grave. I chose well for you when I brokered that match. You now have two fine sons bearing his name, and he lives on through them. We must honour his instructions to the letter.

---

9. Armour protecting the neck. Fighting in heavy armour soon brought on dehydration and knights had to stop often to slake their thirst.

"That stout fellow over there will take good care of Henry as if he was his own. I have seen him bend horseshoes straight and there never was a one to fight with a stave like him.

"He minds me of the story of Little John besting Robin Hood at the river crossing," he chuckled. "Many of my men he has left with a sore pate and grazed knuckles. He will raise him in the ways of a simple country shepherd but we will be nearby and, when we dare, will meet the lad and remind him of his blood ties and birthright.

"Richard leaves tomorrow on the evening tide on a fishing coble that will make its way to Calais. He will stay with my cousin in Guines,[10] who has connections with the French court. He will be under his protection. That means I must take him to the coast tonight if we are to make the morning tide. I suggest you say your goodbyes to him now, without further ado."

Margaret dabbed her tears and smiled weakly at her father. She must be strong and see this thing through, stifling her natural mothering instincts to have her children close at hand. She took Richard by the hand and led him to a corner where she sat with him side by side on a settle. She took a deep breath, in an effort to control her emotions, and presented a serene countenance to her youngest child.

"Richard, you will mind that your father went away to war, to protect all that he held dear? Well, I'm afraid to say that he lost his life fighting for a cause that he believed in."

She looked into his eyes to try and read what sort of reaction this news was met with.

"I know this is very difficult for you to understand at such a tender age but your father loved you dearly and did all he could to protect us. There are some men, some bad men, who would harm us and for that reason, your father left instructions for you to be taken to safety. Your father was a great man and has, *had*," she corrected, "many friends who have pledged to look after you. I want you to be brave, as brave as your father was, and take this journey across the water without any complaint. I truly wish that I could accompany you but I need to stay here to look after our interests. Can you do this for me? Can you be a brave soldier and wait until I come to collect you when things are safe again?"

---

10. Near Calais, which was under English control.

At this, young Richard nodded. "Will Henry be coming with me? If Henry is there I will not be feared of anyone or anything."

Margaret thought for a while how to best answer this. She could hardly say that she needed to keep the two siblings apart so that she had greater chance of keeping a Clifford heir alive.

"Your brother, as brave as he is, suffers from the *mal de mere*. Remember how sick he was when we took him out fishing on the lake? He will have a special hiding place here while you have a great adventure out at sea. Just think of the tales you will have to tell him when you two meet again. Go and say your farewells now for you must leave with your Grandsire presently. I just want you to always remember this. Your father loved you well."

At this Margaret had to look away before her welling emotions betrayed her.

Richard strolled across to part from his brother, Henry, before the journey he must partake. Margaret wondered at what damage these events would have on his young, undeveloped mind. To be uprooted from all he had known was inevitably going to be a trauma, as it would be for an adult. Coupled with the loss of his father and the pursuit of the Yorkists, bent on revenge on the house of Clifford, his personality would be shaped for all his remaining days. Damn and curse this bloody civil strife that had torn England apart!

CHAPTER 5

BOLLING HALL, IN THE COUNTY OF YORK

HERE WAS ENACTED A SCENE THAT WAS to be commonplace across many noble households in the northern counties of England.

Sir Thomas Courtenay had his men pound on the stout oak door of the ancient Pele Tower of Bolling Hall with the butt of their pikes.

A strong patrician voice sounded from within. "Take care; those doors cost my father forty marks. We know why you've come and are full and ready for you."

The bolts slid from the inside and revealed Robert de Bolling, Lord of the manor of Bolling, staring at them with a disinterested manner. He was not over lean or with too much tallow, and had the firm upright stature of a thirty-year-old but his beard was bleached with time. Behind him was his son, Tristram, barely containing his anger, and a large retinue of fair-headed menacing giants, a reminder of the Danes that had once dominated this region.

"Robert de Bolling, gentleman, at your service," drawled Robert as if he had not a care in the world.

Thomas Courtenay, sensing that he had lost the initiative, bellowed at the top of his stentorian voice, "Robert Bolling, Lord of the Manors of Bolling, Chellow …"

"Yes, yes, yes, I know why you have come," replied Robert. "To serve His Majesty King Edward's attainder and evict my household from these lands that we have owned since the time of the Conqueror. I know how it works."

"You are guilty of treason," blustered Sir Thomas. "You have fought against the rightful and noble house of Plantagenet in favour of the heirs of the traitorous House of Lancaster."

"I am fully aware of how this works, Tom," – this said with the emphasis

19

on the knight's name – "but you must clearly understand that we had no choice in the matter. The King, whoever is the King at the time, owns all the lands in the realm. He lets them out to mighty Lords. The mighty Lords let a parcel out to the likes of me, in return for which, I owe them an armed knight if ever they get into conflict. When the time comes, I have to provide an armed knight on a great white charger or forfeit my lands. I hold my land of the Cliffords. They side with the Lancastrians. I have to provide a mounted knight. I am too impoverished to hire one, so I take out my rusty suit of armour and perch on a horse and pretend that I'm the resurrection of the Black Prince, or Richard the Lionheart, or some other such firebrand. All this so that I can feed my family. Now, my good knight, pray tell me how this is an act of treason? I am merely obeying the ancient laws of the land."

"That does not explain why that hulking son of yours donned his sallet and jake and took off to war against his noble and rightful Majesty King Edward," riposted Sir Thomas.

At this, Tristram could hold back no longer and made to speak but was held back by a look from his father.

"You know full well that every man between the ages of fifteen and fifty was conscripted to join the militia, either for the house of Lancaster *or* York, depending on his dwelling place. My lad was no exception. Why would he want to risk his birthright by entering into a bloody fray where none wins? Where is the sense in that?" asked Robert. "The rest of my men you see here were away working in the woods or up on the moors when the recruiting officer arrived and I had no intention of calling them back so that they could die with my Lord Clifford. My son? Clifford knew I had a son and I could not hide the fact from him. He is just a boy, though, and knows nothing of the dispute between kings."

"You will know the wrath and displeasure of my lord and rightful King Edward," Sir Thomas cut in. "He says on this attainder that the Bollings are disgraced and disgraced they will be. You must hereafter leave these lands at the very least. My King will decide whether to take your life."

"I have ever been a loyal subject to the crown, Sir Thomas," was the steady, measured response from Robert, "whomsoever reigns on the throne of our realm. As such, my neck is at the pleasure or displeasure of His Majesty. If he chooses to take it, then how can a simple country gentleman like me gainsay him? My head is here for the chopping block if that is what he desires, but in the meantime, think on this. I will leave my ancestral lands in the corporeal sense, because that is what the King desires. My heart, however, will never give them up. I will reside nearby with Sir Walter Calverley and keep a watchful eye on what is mine by birth. When the King's ire abates, I will be ready to plead my suit for the return of this estate."

Tristram marvelled at his father's composure. Where others boasted and blustered, he was steadfast and quietly went about getting his own way. That was how the estate had grown under his supremacy, acquiring a manor house here and a sheep moor there, always being careful to keep the church on his side with generous contributions to their coffers. Bolling wasn't a big or wealthy estate in the manner of the great lords, but Robert was a man of standing in the community. He made good profit from his fleeces with the burgeoning wool trade in Europe and sold his grain to the townsfolk of Bradford. The Bollings had long been the King's stewards in the area and collected dues from the market, since it had been granted a royal charter.

The great hall in which they stood had been built as a defence against the marauding Scots, a fine old stone tower and a reminder to all that the family held power in the region. The living quarters that abutted the tower were housed in a huge timber-framed manor house, built from oaks felled in the parklands that had been used for hunting since the time of the Conqueror. The family might be cast aside by this new king but everyone knew who the rightful owners to this land were. Any usurpers would be met with hostility. Respect had to be earned the hard way, just as Robert's ancestors had.

"So it is adieu, my Lord Courtenay," smiled Robert, "and you know where to find me if the King so desires. I will take what is left of my meagre possessions and my men and retire to Calverley Hall with my good friend, Sir Walter."

The small group headed for the stables whilst Thomas Courtenay and his men observed the proceedings, bristling for an excuse to draw swords. The Bolling party mounted their horses and headed off down the hill in the direction of Calverley, with many a backward glance at what they were leaving behind.

It was a long, dreary journey in foul, bitter weather, with the prevailing wind driving horizontal rain into their eyes, partly blinding them. Robert bid

21

them all be of good cheer and spoke with confidence of their return, one day soon. A confidence that was unfounded and yet he knew in his heart of hearts that he must return. He could not bear to see his son and heir landless and without honour. It was his destiny to make all good with the world again.

CHAPTER 6

THOMAS LAWKLAND - LONDESBOROUGH, ON THE YORKSHIRE WOLDS

Joseph, Joseph, in your cattle stall,

Joseph, Joseph, what do you make of it all, make of it all?

You and your working man's hands and your wrinkled eyes:

How come that you understand? How come so wise?

How come that you show no surprise

When all around the snowy ground is golden tonight, this frosty night?

How come that you know just who the baby is this winter midnight?

Jake Thackray
© Leola Music Limited

THAT WAS WHEN IT REALLY STARTED. WHEN I was given charge of young Henry Clifford. Just me, my wife, Bess, and my other two boys, Luke and Ralph. Just us five, with half the world trying to hunt us down to find the son of Blackface Clifford.

"Treat him just like your own," entreated my Lady Margaret; "bring him up like a shepherd boy, wild and rough. There must *not* be any visible signs of his birth, for many would hunt him down and harm him. I am giving this, my most precious gift, into your safekeeping," this said with a most beseeching look that deflected straight from my eyes into the depths of my soul.

She need not have said that. I would have done it anyway. I would have done it for most men, but most especially for my Lord Clifford. I had given him my word and I am not an oath-breaker. I had surrendered my own post as one of the most important Reeves, on one of the biggest estates in the realm,

23

for that of a lowly shepherd. A post that suited me nonetheless, as that is how I had started out in life. If I was to raise the lad in the ways of a shepherd, then he need no better master.

"Now then young 'un," I smiled at him, "what shall we do with thee? Tha' shall have to lose that name for a start. We don't want folk calling out Henry, and tha' jumping out from the bushes saying 'here I am'."

"Moses," said Bess. "Moses. He was found in the bulrushes as he had to escape bad folk but he grew up to lead his nation. Moses. A good biblical, God-fearing name."

I looked at Luke and Ralph. They nodded. Bess had been Henry's wet-nurse when Luke was born and the two boys were already good friends. As much as a noble and a commoner might be.

"Moses it is, then," I grinned. "Moses Lawkland. A fine name for these parts. Moses, tha's now got two brothers and a new Fatha and Mother that's proud of you. You happy with that?"

He never was one for talking much in them days. He just looked up at me and then around the room, taking in his new family, and then nodded.

"You're to be a shepherd," I stated, "and yet you have not the tools for the job. How about you and me making a new crook to fit someone of your size? Or a leg cleek so's you can fasten on to young lambs by their hind leg? I know where I can lay my hands on some dried hazel rods and I'm a dab-hand at carving. Do you want me to show you how to do it? Perhaps you would like to make your own?"

He nodded, still not speaking but looking more animated now. I sent Luke and Ralph off to keep an eye on our new flock while we went off together, me taking his little hand in mine, to make him his shepherd's staff.

He instinctively trusted me and I could just tell that he did. We were going to get on fine. He was but seven years old and needed some safety and stability in his life after all the turmoil that was going on around us. He told me, many years later, that this was an awakening for him. As if his life had not existed before. The sudden departure from the enclosed world of the mighty castle in Skipton to the open air where there were no walls holding him in. The feeling of freedom. The close proximity to all that God had created. The curlews and the peewits swirling in vast skies, the wind blowing across the downs making the grass roll like an ocean, the little beck glistening in the sun and teeming with fish. He was a country lad by instinct, if not by birth, and I was now to shape him in my own image.

"Now, let's cut this stick down to your size. Can you help me with this?" I asked.

He nodded eagerly and reached out for the straight hazel rod and held it out in wonder as one might look at a sword, measuring it for balance.

"Now, I have a piece of ram's horn, or we could carve something out of this block of burred elm. Which would you prefer?" I enquired.

He pointed at the ram's horn and nodded.

"Well, that's got a nice twist in it and will make a good leg cleek. Can you sand this down until it's smooth whilst I carve a peg into this hazel rod?"

He nodded again eagerly and set to work, his little hands scraping away furiously at the rough ridges on the horn. His concentration was extreme.

It was dark by the time we had finished and I oiled the crook for him, giving it a smooth, sleek effect.

"Where's my father?" he asked. The first full sentence he had uttered that day.

"Your father?" I responded, shocked, lamely stalling for time.

"Yes, I know he's been killed and you're to be my father now, but where is he? Where has he gone to?"

I was desperately struggling for inspiration. How was I to handle this? I knelt down, put my hand on his shoulder and pointed up to the sky. It was a bright, cloudless night and all the constellations were visible in the night sky. Orion the Hunter, the plough, the bear and the infinite Milky Way, dazzling us with its intensity.

"See that star, up there?" I asked; "the brightest star in the sky?"

He nodded, his face lit up with the moon and more than a little wonder.

"Well, that's the pole star, where all the bravest people like your father go after they leave this earth. You might not be able to see him but he can certainly see you and he'll make sure that no harm comes to you, or to any of us for that matter. He loves you very much and is ever so proud of you. He was the bravest man that I ever met. Some people will say some bad things about him because they are jealous. Ignore them. It's not true. I can tell you that it's not true.

"But, this has got to be our secret. Understand? We don't want folk knowing he's up there and we don't want folk finding you, and that's why your name's Moses and you're staying with us now until things get back to normal."

At this he nodded, solemnly.

"Hungry?" I asked.

"Starving," he replied with such a grin that I exhaled a sigh of relief. It had been a tense few moments and I reckon I had forgotten to breathe with all that had been going on between us.

"Will it be mutton or rabbit?" he posed, striding out for home with his new stick, catching imaginary lambs that had strayed into the ditch.

"We'll have to wait and see, but last one there gets least meat," I countered, breaking into a run.

He beat me to the door by two full lengths.

CHAPTER 7

SKIPTON CASTLE - ELDROTH

ELDROTH WATCHED THE FIRST BEES OF EARLY spring gorging on the cherry blossom in the courtyard. He was contemplating his next move. The birds had flown. Not a sign of his prey and the castle left empty, save for the old fool, Godfrey, and no one could get any sense out of him.

All Sir Thomas Courtenay had to do was walk in through the gates and declare to no one in particular that the castle and Lord Clifford's estates were forfeit and now belonged to the King. These bastards had been well prepared and had long planned to fly the coop.

He thought this through with the instinct of a bloodhound scenting the trail. Everyone he spoke to was tight-lipped and even the promise of free ale in the tavern drew blank looks from all and sundry. This was a close-knit community all right, and he wasn't going to get much from coercion. He wasn't going to get much change out of anyone whilst he was dressed as the King's man, and Sir Thomas' blustering would not get any more than the scantest information.

Blackface Clifford, the Butcher, was some opponent, even though he was dead. The thought of catching his offspring and dragging them and his whore of a wife to Edward gave him a perverse thrill. He giggled to himself and his shoulders rolled in excitement on his wiry little frame. His nose twitched and rose to take the scent as if he could actually smell their trail, but all that could really be found on the air was the tang of sheep dung. Skipton, or sheep-town, certainly lived up to its name.

His mind turned over and over. He put himself in Clifford's position. If he were to make plans for the safety of his sons, if he was killed or captured in battle, what would he do? If Lady Clifford had to act quickly after his death, where would she go?

There was too much guesswork for the first question, and Clifford was no slouch at outfoxing people, as he had shown at Sandal and Ferrybridge. No, the answer had to be with Margaret Clifford. What would she do? There were probably two answers to that. The first would be to hightail it to a Lancastrian stronghold and ask help of Margaret of Anjou. The second was to run home. Home to her father where she would have an instinctive feeling of safety. That would be his first port of call. He didn't know much about her family and no one here would help him. He would have to go back to York and find out where her family seat was. Might as well report to Edward as well, although that might result in a tongue-lashing for letting the trail go cold.

Still, he was the man for the job and he was determined to hunt them down as much for sheer pleasure as for the bag of gold that would be his reward. He called for his horse and asked Sir Thomas' page to provide him with provisions for his journey.

Edward badly wanted these boys. There was a real old-fashioned blood feud raging between the two sides and Clifford had prosecuted it with more vigour. It had started when Thomas, the eighth Lord Clifford, had been killed by the Duke of York at the battle of St Alban's. The warlike Cliffords would not let the tally stand at that and his son, John, had killed the Duke of York and the young Earl of Arundel at the siege of Sandal Castle. The Yorkist propaganda machine had embellished the tale and embroidered the facts so that Clifford was said to have murdered the young lad in cold blood, despite him pleading for his life. Even Eldroth, who was not there, knew this not to be true and that the lad had been killed in the heat of battle, but this had earned John Clifford the sobriquet of Butcher, or Blackface. He was a fierce bastard though, and was always ready to take the battle to the enemy, as he had when he struck right at the Yorkist vanguard at Ferrybridge.

Only 500 men at his back and he had accounted for the deaths of nearly 3,000 men, mostly drowned in the river. Even though he was long dead, the score was two-one, to John Clifford. Blackface Clifford would be laughing from his grave. Eldroth knew this would rankle with Edward and be eating at his heart and his pride. He wanted the Clifford heirs just as much as he wanted the kingdom. If it were too easy to find them, his reward would be little. He would have to craft his tale for Edward to prise more money out of him.

When all was ready, he spurred the grey mare in the flanks and headed back east on one of the old drovers' roads. He knew most of the highways and byways in the North and had committed them to his memory. He was the sort to squirrel away the minutest detail. That was why he was trusted to cover up the tracks of any of the misdeeds of his betters.

He coaxed the horse into a trot and steadily climbed upland into the moors without a backward glance. It was a fine day. Soon the weather would turn and make for better conditions for his manhunt. He chuckled at the prospect. After three miles he quickly looked around and then reined his horse in to hide behind a clump of gorse. The scrub was now dense and in full yellow bloom. He had good cover and also a high vantage point to see if any one of the villagers had followed him. He was a veteran soldier and had learned his fieldcraft well. After ten minutes he decided that no one was on his trail, bent on doing him mischief, and heaved himself back into the saddle. He let the grizzled mare walk on at her own steady pace, content with the thought of finding a warm tavern for the night and ale paid for by the King.

High on a mossy green ridge, obscured by his flock of sheep, and the sun that Eldroth had been squinting into, was a lone shepherd. His black eyes set in nut-brown skin, heavily etched by the elements.

"Why would someone think he was being followed?" he mused to himself. "Unless he's up to no good."

CHAPTER 9

LONDESBOROUGH, THE YORKSHIRE WOLDS

THWACK! WENT THE STAFF OF YOUNG RALPH Lawkland on to the side of the head of Adam Gill, their chief protagonist.

At thirteen years old, Adam was a full two years older than his opponent and headed up a small but evil gang comprising the Danedike brothers, self-proclaimed toughs of the village. He had taunted the newcomers and mocked their accents, daring them to challenge his supremacy.

Ralph looked at the mean ginger-haired strapling, his face dotted with freckles, and took him at his word. The boy went down like a stunned hog, slaughtered for the table.

He squealed like one too, making enough noise to raise the dead.

"There was no need to 'it me," he wailed in between sobs and piggy squeals, snot streaming from his nose and blood seeping from his right ear.

"Then why did tha' ruddy ask for it?" snapped Ralph. "Now get up and clear off, or I'll gi' thee another!"

One of the Danedike brothers stepped forward, seemingly unfazed by the fate of his friend. Rather than confront Ralph though, he roughly pushed Henry's shoulder. He was clearly older than Henry and looked like someone who was used to taking a knock and giving it back with interest.

"Tha' brother's stoved Adam's 'ead in wi' a stick but ah bet tha' can't fight wi' tha' fists," he challenged.

Henry pushed him back, gingerly. The Danedike boy pushed even harder, knocking Henry back a few paces. Ralph watched on, his staff clenched in his fist, but did nothing.

"Think tha's up to it then?" he persisted at Henry, making two fists and circling round him, balancing his weight from one foot to the other. He deliberately placed himself so that Henry was between him and Ralph with the fearsome stick.

From nowhere, he jabbed a punch at Henry's eye and followed through with a whippy punch to his solar plexus.

"Stop him," pleaded Luke to Ralph. "He's a head taller than our Moses."

Ralph gestured forbiddingly at Luke. "He must learn to fight 'is own battles. Fatha says he mun be toughened up, like."

"It's not a fair fight," pleaded Luke.

At this, Henry connected with a combination of punches to this feisty protagonist and one punch emitted a resounding crack of fist against head-bone. This had no lasting effect though. The boy, momentarily stunned, shook it off and responded with a double-fisted blow. Henry was poleaxed and fell heavily into the mud, retching and heaving, his left eye so swollen that it closed.

"He'll be better for a beatin' and will fight keener next time," Ralph explained to Luke as the Danedike gang sniggered and turned back home, strutting down the lane.

The pathetic, heaving bundle that was Henry metamorphosed into a blur of fury that leapt off the ground and vaulted on to his enemy's retreating back. The bigger boy shrugged him off with a backwards jab of his elbow but Henry spun him round, face-on, and delivered a thrusting upwards punch into his windpipe. The boy gasped for breath, choking and holding his throat. His guard thus abandoned made him an easy target for Henry who kicked him full in the stomach and, as he reeled sideways, heeled him in the thigh. He fell, sprawling and scrambling in the road, the damaged quadricep rendering the leg useless.

Henry grabbed for the next boy, his anger now at fever pitch. He grasped him by his lank hair and swung him to the ground. "Now, will you kneel before me, you churl?" snarled Henry, intent on the total subjugation of all who stood in his path. His Clifford blood had surfaced and he was bent on a crushing revenge.

He was pulled violently backwards by the strong, firm grip of Ralph.

"None of that talk round here," rebuked Ralph through gritted teeth, "or we'll all be for the drop. Aren't we in danger enough?"

"Where did you learn to fight like that?" marvelled Luke.

"Father's soldiers taught me a few tricks," acknowledged Henry modestly, then, more boldly, "you should see what damage I can do with a short sword."

All the commotion had attracted the attention of the villagers, not that fighting boys were an unusual sight, but there was a common understanding that they must not do anything that would draw attention to their new neighbour. Sir Henry Bromflete would not hesitate in punishing them severely if the boy's presence was betrayed. Not that he need do that as they would be naturally tight-lipped to the enquiries of any outsiders.

Tom Lawkland followed hard on the heels of the villagers, his countenance betraying a look of thunder living just under his skin, about to erupt at any more signs of provocation.

"Keep them lads of your'n under check, will you, Harry Danedike," he demanded. "I'll not tell thee again, I'll let one of Sir Henry's men explain it to thee at the point of a halberd. There's real danger about. One of the shepherds over by Skipton reckons the King's spies are at large. He lit a beacon for the next dale on, and so forth, and so it's been relayed to me. We'll 'ave them all snooping and poking round here afore long and when they do, all they'll see is our Moses, looking no different from his brothers, tending sheep and chewing on a blade of grass. Is that clear?" He looked around him from man to woman and woman to man, letting the message sink in with the force of his personality and brooding presence.

"Nay, we understand full well, Tom," offered one of the men, "it's that Danedike family that allus causes bother. They can no more control them lads than tha' can stop a pig rolling in mud."

At this, Harry Danedike made to answer but Tom stayed him with the raised open palm of his hand.

"Enough of this chelp[11]. We need some harmony in this village. We need you all to understand what's at stake. We're all in this together, like it or not. If King Edward discovers that we're harbouring that poor lad here, we'll all be up for the drop o' York,[12] make no mistake. So think on. Keep your differences to yourselves until this all blows over."

---

11. Cheek or chatter.
12. The gallows.

Tom took Henry by the shoulder and shepherded him through the parting crowd.

"Come on, our Moses, there's sheep that need dagging and it'll not get done standing round 'ere. You two," – with a sharp look at Ralph and Luke – "you can come too. I'd rather 'ave you somewheres where I can keep an eye on you."

When they were out of earshot he enquired, "So, what 'appened then, boys?" This said at the more pliable Luke, pointedly ignoring the taciturn Ralph and the brooding, seething Henry.

"Our Ralph walloped that big ginger lummox wi' 'is stick, cause he were picking a fight. Fair cracked 'is 'ead open and he squealed like a farrowing sow. Then one o' them Danedike bruisers picked on our Henry – sorry, Moses – and Ralph made 'im go it alone. I thought 'e were gonna get a pasting but 'e cleaned 'im up like the slaughter man. There's no doubt who's cock o' the village lads now; it's the Lawkland brothers," he beamed, smiling up at his father to reveal his missing front milk teeth.

Despite himself, Tom could not suppress a chuckle.

Tom tousled his hair. "Let's hope tha's got some energy left for working the sheep. Weather's warming up and they want fettling afore it's time for a proper shearing. Can thy handle these sheep, they're a tad bigger than tha's used to?"

The longwool sheep on the Wolds were a bigger breed than the Dalesbred sheep the boys were familiar with. The warmer climate and verdant pasture nurtured a breed that yielded softer wool and provided a bigger meat carcass. Tom thought to himself that he'd take some back with him to try out in the lower pastures, when he eventually returned home to his beloved Dales. Whenever that was.

"Right you two swaggering peacocks, get tha' shears and get to work in the top fold. I've not had an honest day's work outta thee since we got here. Moses, tha' can come wi' me."

He steered Henry towards the lower fold where he had rounded up a goodly number of ewes, their lambs bleating at their sides.

"Right lad, tha's not done any dagging afore, by my reckoning, so hark on at what I'm about to tell thee. Tha's to cut shitty wool off a sheep's arse or it'll end up wi' blowfly. Tha' dun't want thee sheep getting blowfly or tha'll have a lot of work on thee hands. Blowfly is when flies lay their eggs in the sheeps' mucky arse and they hatch as maggots and eat its flesh. Now I knaws it might not be a natural job for a high-born gentleman like thee but tha's a shepherd now and tha's got to do what a shepherd 'as to do. Even one that's a fighting cock," he laughed.

Henry clearly contemplated the task ahead with the greatest of distaste but he knew that his very survival depended on blending in with these rough, rustic folk and their struggle against nature for subsistence.

Tom grabbed a sheep by the neck and held it steady, astride its torso with his legs dug into its ribs. Every struggle resulted in his strong knees kneading into its side to subdue any movement until the beast calmed down with the sound of his soothing voice.

He tried to make things easier for Henry by reciting a poem that he normally reserved for shearing time in the summer:

"How meek, how patient, the mild creature lies!
What softness in its melancholy face,
What dumb complaining innocence appears!
As I wield the blade of grace
But it is not horrid slaughter that is o'er you waved;
No, 'tis the tender swain's well guided shears,
Who having now, to pay his annual care,
Borrows your fleece, to you a cumbrous load,
Will send you bounding to your hills again."

Traditional poem

"No hills around this place lad, are there? Not like our homeland is it? But home it will be to us for a long while yet, god willing."

Henry responded with a smile of quiescence. They were in this together.

"Keep still, me bonny lass," said Tom to the ewe. "We'll soon have thee cleaned up and out wi' the lambs chewing on that new pasture. Now, Moses, grab them shears and cut them dags off, be careful tha' don't cut her flesh. These beasts are our living."

Henry grimaced and set to the task with a gritty countenance. He was so fearful of cutting the helpless animal that his focus precluded any thoughts of what he was touching and he soon became adept at the job as Tom caught sheep after sheep for his ministrations.

"Tha's a natural," conceded Tom, relaxing now that he knew his charge would not baulk at the task in hand. "It must be difficult for thee, I knaws. I've been thinking on what must be going through your 'ead. I don't rightly know, as I've not had your upbringing, but if I were thee I'd be in a right old state. Worried about your mother and your grandfatha and your brother across the seas. And you end up here with the likes o' me, when you could have been a great lord had it not been for that battle down the road.

"But I'll tell thee this. Next to being a Lord o' the realm, being a shepherd comes a close second. You are the leader of your flock and lord of all the hills you survey, as far as your eyes can see. The sheepdog is your trusty lieutenant and guards against the wolves that would threaten your kingdom. He marshals tha' forces for thee at shearing and at lambing times like you're preparing for a mighty battle, running them down the hill wherever you bid them to go.

"The sheep pay tribute and tithe to you with their wool and flesh. These sheepskins protect us from the winter cold. Aye, being a shepherd is a good occupation. Mark my words though, it's hard work and you will have to work on tha' skills as hard as any squire labours for his knight. Do you think tha's up to it young fellow?"

Henry, who by now was quite pleased that he could execute his task with accomplishment, nodded and let a smile escape. A smile that was the smile of a country boy, happy with his lot. He had made good progress since the turmoil of the flight from Skipton Castle. If this was to be his life, there was no point rebelling against it. He might as well do as he was bid with good heart and enjoy the care of these simple, well-meaning folk.

Tom continued. "Now these 'ere sheep. They're bonny enough but they'd not last five minutes up in the Dales on a bad winter's night. Sheep up there can live offa thin air and survive bad weather when others don't. They don't need penning in fields and enclosures either, they're hefted to farmer's hill. That means they don't wander off on to someone else's moor, causing the shepherd a load of work. They know where they're meant to bide and that's where they stay. When snow's bad they'll come down fells for some hay without sheep dogs even chasing 'em. We's even got our own language, did thee know that, young Moses?"

Henry shook his head, continuing with his work, looking up from time to time into Tom's watchful eyes.

"Aye, for instance, we don't count in English fashion. We use a language that were here since before the Romans came, and each Dale 'as its own variety, like. I were taught by a Swaledale shepherd and this is how it goes," he sighed, lilting into an ancient chant that was soothing like a lullaby.

"Yan, tan, tether, mether, pip. Azer, sezar, akker, conter, dick. Yanadick, tanadick, tetheradick, metheradick, bumfit. Yanabum, tanabum, tetherabum, metherabum, jiggitt."

"That's twenty," calculated Henry. "What happens after twenty?"

"Why, tha' picks up a stone and starts again till you gets to hold another stone. Clever folk us shepherds, tha' knows," he winked.

Henry asked him to repeat it. Soon, he had the task mastered, chanting it in a sing-song alto voice that would put the choristers at York to shame. It had such a soothing quality that it made the dismal work seem like a pleasure.

He was still chanting it to himself after his supper, when he lay in his bed, alongside his new brothers in arms.

CHAPTER 9

ELDROTH,
DROVERS PATH,
SOMEWHERE NEAR HELMSLEY,
EAST RIDING OF YORKSHIRE

ELDROTH SMILED TO HIMSELF AS HE DROVE a herd of twenty roan cattle down the old drovers' route to Londesborough. It was a fine spring day and the hedgerow birds were busy gathering food for their young. A blackbird trilled its sweet melodic song from a hawthorn, whilst a mistle-thrush filled its beak with worms ready to fill the needy mouths of its hatchlings.

As predicted, Edward was livid that the Clifford heirs had escaped his grasp. Eldroth had tried to explain that such a prey was not going to be easy to seize but it was a full ten minutes before the magisterial wrath had abated. It was his insinuating brother, Richard, who suggested he extend the search by employing other hunters and proffering a generous reward. This caused something of a commotion with the assembled throng, not least of which from William Stanley, a covetous man with a dubious reputation for intrigue. The grasping Lord Stanley jumped at the chance but Edward, sure of his man, was prepared to hear Eldroth out.

"Your Majesty, we need stealth and not strength for this sortie," he explained. "By my reckoning, the Clifford woman will be with her father, the Baron of Vescy, at Londesborough now. She will have the brats hidden somewhere nearby. My plan is this. Your Majesty sends Sir Thomas Courtenay and his entourage to make formal enquiries of their whereabouts. I will stay in the region, masquerading as a cattle drover, watching and waiting. She is unlikely to admit anything to Sir Thomas and come out with some sort

37

of subterfuge, but I will stay in the area. Once he has left, she will follow a mother's instinct and check that her chicks are safe. I will be there to watch the proceedings and thus will I flush out the coop."

"What detains you, Eldroth?" demanded Edward. "Make haste before the trail goes cold and the brats reach sword-bearing age."

"Money, Sire," was the sly response. "Expenses. I can't be a cattle-drover without cattle and I'll need a good dog to guard them, and a pack-horse…"

Edward rose from his chair and threw a purse of gold coins at his feet. "Now, out of my sight. I don't want to see you again until you have the brats bound together in chains."

So, as he ambled down the road, idly flicking the rump of the nearest heifer with a switch, he sniggered to himself. He had requisitioned the cattle in the name of the King, intimidating the poor farmer into submission, the gold still safely in his purse. The dog he had bought was a beauty, part mastiff, just the job for guarding the cattle while he was doing his surveillance elsewhere. He had used big bull-mastiffs in the French campaigns when he was terrorizing the paysans. The big dogs made up for his own lack of stature, and all you had to do was to get them to bare their slavering, slobby fangs and the peasants soon yielded up their hidden gold.

Now all he had to do was act the part of a cattle drover. A Welsh cattle drover, he thought. He had lived amongst enough Welsh archers to imitate their lilting accent. What name though? Ifor, Ieuan, Trefor, Mervyn? No, not quite right. Gwillam? That sounded more like it. "Gwillam the Welsh Cattle Drover from Clwyd, at your ser-fice," he said out loud, getting into character. This was the part of the job he loved best. Deceiving people. Then, the look in their eyes when they realized they were duped. This would often result in their sudden death, and there would probably be some blood spilt during this adventure, but this time he had to bring the boys out alive. This was only likely to be a temporary state of affairs, though, and he was likely to get the job of despatching them once they had served Edward's purpose. "More wages of sin," he chortled, with that strange rolling of his skinny weasel shoulders. During times of war and strife, dark characters like him always profited.

On the second day of his journey he brought the cattle to a halt on a ridge overlooking Brough Castle. This would be a good vantage point to watch the comings and goings at the castle once Sir Thomas and his useless retinue arrived.

Also, he could keep an eye on the villagers below. He made sure the beasts had plenty of pasture so that they would not wander, then set the dog to guard them while he carried out his undercover reconnaissance in the tiny village.

The tavern was as good a place to start as any. The smoky room went quiet when he entered and one of the drinkers spat on the floor before uttering, "not just any off-becomed'un, but a bloody Welshman at that, by the look of 'is cloak."

"Ye-ess, my friend, but a Welshman as is buy-ing the drinks, see? My name's Gwillam and I'fe 'ad a long jour-ney and am in need of some of your good English ale," he said, with a rising inflection at the end of his sentence.

"What's thou after then?" queried his antagonist.

"Just some ad-fice on where I can get the best price for my catt-el. Now, who would like to join me?" asked Eldroth, who soon had them in his grip, using the store cupboard of jokes and anecdotes he had garnered on his travels. Most of the villagers had not ventured much further than a few hamlets away and he soon had them in his thrall, taking every one in to his confidence whilst assessing them for any noteworthy traits or clues that might lead to his quarry.

One fellow had a livid, fresh scar running diagonally across his face. A recent veteran of the battle of Towton, no doubt. One of the few that had escaped the slaughter and returned home. He would exploit this when the time came.

"Had an accident, my friend?" he insinuated. "What's your name?"

The man, startled from his reverie, looked shocked and took a while before he could muster a response.

"This?" he said pointing to his scar, forcing a smile. "Nothing more than a cut from an overhanging bramble in the coppice over yonder. The name's Martin, by the way. I'm helping out the shepherd round here. There's plenty of work on for them as wants it."

The following day, Sir Thomas arrived. From his hilltop vantage, Eldroth watched the proceedings as the search party approached Brough Castle.

"Open in the name of the King!" Thomas bellowed. He was admitted with his men as Eldroth knew he would be, and after less than an hour the men left the castle for the tavern, Sir Thomas taking up lodgings in the castle for the night, presumably.

As the afternoon faded, Eldroth got what he wanted. A fine-looking lady opened the west-facing door, looked from side-to-side, then scurried, unaccompanied, to a large farm house beyond the village.

When she departed, Eldroth made his move. He strode purposefully to the dwelling and then slowed down his pace to a saunter as he approached. He was surprised to see scarface Martin, loading a haycart, but merely smiled his recognition and asked if his master was in. When he had elicited his name and whereabouts from Martin, he made for the baling shed where the fleeces were stored. He made a mental note of all the buildings, the terrain, the farm dogs that were barking about the place. He had enough experience from France to know how to reconnoitre a homestead like this and maximize his chances of plunder.

"Master Lawkland?" he mewed at the doorstep, peering into the dusty building.

"Who wants to know?" demanded the large figure of Tom, looming out of the darkness at the far corner of the wattle and daub barn.

"Gwillam, the cattle drover," Eldroth lisped. "I have these lovely catt-el, see, and I was wondering whether a fine gentleman like you, as lives in this big 'ouse, would be interested in some prime Welsh beef?"

"If tha's not blind, tha' can see this is a sheep farm. I've no use for cattle and folks as lives round here can't afford 'em. You'll not get a good price this side o' York," was the terse response.

"The market's buggered since the bloody war. The price of everything's gone up so's as folk can't afford 'em and I can't get enough labour to 'elp shear the sheep and cut the hay for the winter fodder," he continued.

Eldroth took in the tousle-headed boys helping Tom. Like the shepherd, they had not stopped their work at his entrance, but occasionally shot a glance in his direction.

"Lovely looking lads you've got there," offered Eldroth. "All three yours?"

Tom nodded by way of a response.

Eldroth took them in more keenly; all three had straw-coloured hair but one had darker eyes than the others, almost black, where the other two had the pale blue eyes of their father. The dark-eyed boy had a prominent widow's peak on his forehead and was of a sturdier build, whilst the other two were more wiry. That was at least one of the Clifford brats, no doubt about it.

"That one there looks a bit different; your wife not been keeping someone else's bed warm while you've spent the night out lambing?" ventured Eldroth.

This was met with a violent start from Tom, grasping Eldroth by the jerkin and lifting him clean off his feet until he was eyeball to eyeball, so close that he could smell his feral breath.

"No off-ence, no off-ence," gurgled Eldroth, "it's only my Welsh humour, see?"

Tom stared at him for another full minute before slowly letting him down to his feet.

"That boy, that boy is the spit-drawn image of his grandsire, the best breeder of sheepdogs in the East Riding," growled Tom. "If you were from round these parts you'd know that. Now don't you go blackening the name of my good wife or you'll end up roasted on a spit."

Eldroth mumbled his apologies, bowed and left, secretly chuckling to himself. The man, although clearly a Yorkshireman, did not have an East Riding accent, and the whelp was definitely a Clifford by his thick thatch of hair and widow's peak. Edward had described the family characteristics full well.

That night, he made his move on Martin.

"That scar can get you into trouble, see?" insisted Eldroth. "There's plenty of the King's soldiers about with Sir Thomas and you could easily get arrested for fighting for the Lancastrians."

Martin, who had drunk deep from his cups, looked befuddled and scared.

"Now, I'm your friend and will protect you, even give you gold if you help me, but I need you to do something for me," wheedled Eldroth.

Martin stared at him blankly.

Eldroth persisted. "I need you to help me get to Tom Lawkland's farm without setting the dogs off barking. They know you and won't bark when they see you approach."

Martin sat bolt upright and looked incredulously at Eldroth. "But, my master..." he stuttered.

Eldroth did not allow him to finish. "Do you know what Edward does to Lancastrians who have raised arms against him? He beheaded forty knights at Towton rather than sell them for ransom, and they were gentlemen. Do you know what he does to common soldiers?" menaced Eldroth.

The young man, clearly mortified, made no response.

Eldroth pushed a small bag of gold into his hand. "Now, lead the way, Master Martin."

Eldroth laughed at his own duplicity. He had a flair for intimidation and intrigue and thought through the night's proceedings as they walked together to the farmstead.

Foolish Martin would meet his death once he had silenced the dogs, with a knife in his back. He'd get his bag of gold back. Once in the house, he'd slit the throat of the big bastard shepherd. Normally he would take pleasure of the woman before he sent her to her Maker but there was no time for that tonight. His thoughts went to all the nuns he'd raped and killed in Normandy and Picardy. He always used the same line: "You might be the bride of Christ, but tonight you're my whore," as he ripped off their linen smocks and jiggled their breasts. He was going to hell in a handcart, that was for sure. Killing them was a mercy as they'd never live with the disgrace anyway. Still, there might be time for a quick feel of Mistress Lawkland before slitting her throat. He giggled at the thought, convulsively wriggling his round shoulders. The boy would get bundled into a sack and then strapped to the pack horse he'd got waiting nearby. He'd steal one of Sir Thomas' horses to make a speedy retreat. The pompous bastard would kick up a fuss but Edward would forgive him anything for one of the Clifford boys. Once the brat was in Edward's custody he'd use him as a bargaining plea to wheedle out the whereabouts of his brother from Lady Margaret. It was gratifying to do something in life you really enjoyed, and get lots of gold for it too.

"Go stand there by the woolshed while I quieten the dogs," whispered Martin in a slurred voice. The dogs approached, wagging their tails and snuffling against the staggering, drunken Martin, while Eldroth lingered patiently in the shadows.

Next, total darkness. Strong arms had reached Eldroth from behind and pulled a woolsack over his head down to his elbows. He struggled and bellowed but was dragged with his feet scraping across the floor, as if he were a child's rag doll.

"Light the lamp," commanded a deep, rough voice. Eldroth was heaved off his feet and deposited into a deep pit. The sack was lifted from his head and he blinked to take in the surroundings. The big shepherd was standing over him while Martin, fully restored to his sober self, took up a spade and started filling in the gaps around Eldroth with dirt, packing it in tightly. At first Eldroth thought he was to be buried alive, and screamed, but the soil only came up to his chin.

Tom Lawkland stood there impassively, not saying a word as Eldroth was encased in his earthy prison.

"Help, get me out of here!" shrieked Eldroth. "I'm the King's man and his soldiers are all round here."

"I know who you are and what you are," Tom calmly stated, "and you can scream all you like as no one will hear you here apart from the screech owls and other creatures of the night. Creatures you will be familiar with as you occupy the same dark, murky place."

"I've got gold, I've got cattle. I'll take you to it if you only let me go," wheedled Eldroth. "I won't inform on you if you only let me go."

"I'm not bothered for gold, and as for your cattle, I've already told you, I'm purely a sheep man. What I want from you is information," menaced Tom.

"What? I don't know anything. I was just…" spluttered Eldroth, but Tom cut across him.

"Every man has his breaking point, be it a hot iron, a sharp blade flensing the skin, or other diverse tortures, and I'll try them all out on you to get what I want," spat Tom, kneeling down on his haunches to press his skinning knife against Eldroth's nose.

He watched his prisoner for a while, trying to penetrate what went on behind his eyes and then turned to Martin. "Get me the rat cage, will you?"

Eldroth's eyes flickered, and for the first time betrayed real fear.

"Yes, the rats should do it," he said as he lowered the cage over Eldroth's head. The captive wriggled now, clenching his buried fists, trying to extend his elbows to loosen the earth's grip, but it was futile.

Tom laughed. "Now, you tell me all you know, answer each question one by one. For every lie you tell me I'll add a rat to your cage They've not been fed since you got here the other day. They've been waiting for you and they're hungry."

43

Eldroth's eyes darted to meet his jailer, furious that his subterfuge had been so easily detected.

"You'll get nothing from me, you big hairy bastard!" he boasted, but his bombast soon turned to a shriek as a rat was dangled by its tail and dropped into the cage

He screamed like all the nuns that he'd raped. He squealed like the children he'd spitted on the end of his halberd. He tried to writhe in his loamy prison but there was no escape.

"I'll tell, I'll tell, just get the thing away from me!" he screeched.

"I'll take it away *after* you've told me all I want to know," smiled the shepherd.

Eldroth confessed all. His work for the House of York. The King's grisly intentions for the Clifford boys. The bounty offered to Lords Courtenay and Stanley to hunt them down. He would have sold his own mother just to get away from the proximity of the rat, with its evil eyes, twitching whiskers and yellow teeth.

When all was said, Tom motioned Martin to fetch something. It was a flask of wine.

That was the last earthly thing Eldroth saw as Tom smothered his head with a fleece, gently leeching the life out of him. As soon as he was dead, Martin removed the earth and helped heave the lifeless form from its temporary grave.

"Looks like he was right handed," said Tom as he clinically examined the hands of the corpse. Martin clasped Eldroth's fingers around the flask and held it there until rigor mortis had set in.

"Right, not a mark on him," stated Tom, grimly satisfied with his night's work. "We'll heave him into Helvin Bog before dawn and he'll be there for all to see as a wandering drunk as has lost 'is footing."

And thus did Eldroth end his days. The evil assassin, pillager, raper of nuns, despoiler of children, gone to meet his Maker by the fleece of one of God's meekest creatures.

High on the ridge, Eldroth's dog howled, baying at the moon and to anyone that would listen, at the exact same time of his master's earthly departure.

CHAPTER 10

HOB HILL FARM, LONDESBOROUGH

"Is HE GONE?" ENQUIRED BESS LAWKLAND, AT first startled as Tom walked through the door, then relieved it was her husband and not the horrid little man that had encroached upon the quiet life of the village.

Tom looked at her sweet face by the soft glow of the tallow candles she was now busy lighting, careworn with all the stress of the last few days. She had thought them all safe here. After all, this was the village where she was born and had always relied on as a safe haven. The incursion of others was a rarity and a violation of the peace, tranquillity and rhythm of their pastoral life. Lady Margaret, also native-born and with her child at stake, must be feeling the same way.

He nodded and smiled in an effort to reassure her. "Gone to meet St Peter," he said, raising his eyes upwards, "only to be cast down to meet old Nick down below," he gestured at the ground. "And there'll be the devil to pay when he's found missing. This business is not over yet," he paused. "We've put 'im in the bog so's that it looks like an accident, like he fell in drunk. There's not a mark on 'im and he's holding a wine flask in his hand, so we hope it's reckoned on as an accident. Let's pray to the Lord that it is."

Bess tiptoed over to watch the slumbering boys. She had been Henry's wet nurse, delighted that she had given birth to Luke at the same time as Margaret had produced Henry as the heir to the Cliffords. It was only natural that Margaret would choose the maid she had brought from her village, someone she had known all her life, to suckle the infant. And now Bess had to raise him as her own and indeed, she dearly loved him as she did her own two boys, notwithstanding the risk she was undertaking. A dog howling out in the night made her shudder and brought her back to the present.

45

"What's to do next?" she enquired anxiously.

"There's nowt much we can do until dawn. We need to tell Sir Henry what's occurred and then see what's to be done from there. If we send a message to 'im in the middle o' the night, we shall be attracting too much attention. I shall 'ave to send Martin in come dawn, wi' some lamb chops or summat for 'is Lordship's breakfast so's he can get a message to 'im. Until then, we hold fast here. Best get some sleep, love, there's no point fretting about what can't be helped."

Tom looked lovingly at his wife, her silky fair hair part obscuring her beautiful violet, doe-like eyes. What had they got themselves into? He stroked her hair and looked into her eyes and made to reassure her. He knew this was a bad business and that they'd likely be on the move again come morning, but there was no point in worrying Bess with that information.

When she had finally nodded off into a fitful sleep, Tom started preparing for yet another journey, a flight from those who would harm an innocent child and all who harboured him. He packed as many provisions as he thought they could carry without being too burdened as to impede their speed. Some protection against the elements was needed if they could not find shelter for the night. A flint, striking iron and tinder to make fire. Preserved food, securely wrapped in parcels to last them for a week or more. The boys would have to carry some of the burden, but how would Bess cope with such a journey? Such a journey? Why, he did not even know where they were bound. All he knew was that this was now a dangerous place. Their cover blown in a week or two, if not already. And in the dank night air, Eldroth's dog howled at the crescent moon as if he were one of the hounds of hell pursuing them to their doom.

Next morning, Tom went about his work as usual whilst Martin took the message in to Brough Castle at the same time as the bakers entered with their fresh supply of bread and pastries for the household. It was not long before Sir Henry himself arrived, with a very worried look on his countenance.

Without any preamble, he urged, "You must get out of here without delay. It's too dangerous for you to stay. I'll have a packhorse brought across here within the hour. You'll have two mounted archers to escort you to the border of my lands. You must leave for the sake of the boy; his mother is beside herself with worry. I've already hastened my fastest rider off to Cumbria, to

Sir Lance Threlkeld's estate, to tell them of your coming. You'll be so far out of the way as to be safe there. The journey will not be an easy one, though."

Tom looked him straight in the eye and nodded.

"I'm forgetting my manners with all this haste," said Sir Henry in a softer tone. "I am indebted to you as indeed are all my family. Thank you for what you have done, and done right well. That man was a hired assassin according to young Martin?"

At this Tom nodded again.

Sir Henry gripped him by the arm. "John Clifford chose his man well when he chose you to be Henry's guardian. You are as brave as any knight."

"Aye, well. Talk's cheap," retorted Tom grimly. "Lad's not safe yet by a long shot and there's a job to be done."

Sir Henry smiled ruefully. "Yes, you're right, and Lady Margaret will not have a moment's peace until she hears that you have arrived safe and well. I must go to her now and prepare for what's about to unfold here in the dark days to come. I bid you adieu, Master Tom, and God speed you on your journey."

At this, Sir Henry mounted his horse stiffly and kicked it into a canter back in the direction of the castle.

***

Meanwhile, the villagers were waking to the blood-curdling howls and yapping of the dog on the ridge. It was not long before this attracted the attention of the King's soldiers.

"Go and see what's happening to that cursed hound," demanded the Captain to one of his men.

The soldier reluctantly climbed the ridge to where the mad dog was baying, whilst the cattle chewed at the sweet spring pasture, apparently oblivious to the commotion.

The dog would not let the soldier any more than twenty yards close to Eldroth's encampment. He circled round, hallooing and calling out for someone to keep the beast quiet, but there was no sign of life. The campfire looked long dead. He trudged wearily back down the hill.

"I don't like the smell of this," observed the Captain, when he had heard the soldier's report. "There's something wrong here. Go at once to Sir Thomas and tell him I sent you. Tell him what you have seen."

Indeed, Sir Thomas Courtenay was of the same opinion as the Captain when he arrived.

"Why would he leave his cattle overnight, free for anyone to steal away? No, this is a pretty parcel, I'll be bound. These bastards here have something to do with this. I'll see what Sir Henry has to say about this affair."

He turned as he strode back to his horse. "Now shoot that bloody cur will you, I can't hear myself think."

The Captain gesticulated towards one of his archers. The man pulled on his drawstring and unsheathed a single arrow. Taking aim, he loosed a bodkin that went straight, clean through the poor demented creature's skull. It fell to the ground with barely a whimper.

CHAPTER 11

BROUGH CASTLE, LONDESBOROUGH

"MY LORD HENRY!" BELLOWED SIR THOMAS IN his trademark pompous manner.

"Yes?" responded Sir Henry, looking up from his plate of mutton chops and coddled eggs.

"What do you know of a cattle drover? On the King's business, no less."

"A cattle drover? I know nothing of such people," replied a bemused-looking Henry.

"Well, make it your business to know. He's gone missing. Gone missing on your land and if he's not found I'll hold you personally responsible," said Thomas with more than a hint of glee in his voice.

"This is madness," was Sir Henry's response. "How am I to know of cattle drovers coming through my land? Such peasants move their beasts across the countryside without let or hindrance. It's an ancient right. Why should I concern myself with such matters?"

"I trust you are as innocent in this matter as you make out," intoned Sir Thomas. "As I say, this was not just any cattle drover, but one on the King's business."

"What would a cattle drover be doing on the King's business?" replied a seemingly puzzled Sir Henry, still eating his breakfast.

"That I cannot disclose," Thomas retorted sharply. "Nonetheless, he is to be found or there will be the devil to pay. He was in the employ of His Majesty, King Edward.

"I suspect there is mischief afoot. If he has come to any harm, His Majesty will bring the suspects to account – and you are a suspect." This was said with a sharp look in Henry's direction to gauge a reaction.

"A suspect, me? How am I a suspect when I know not of what you are talking? I am powerless in this matter. What would you have me do?"

Sir Thomas pondered for a moment. "Find him. He has gone missing on your lands. Find him and bring him to me by nightfall or it will be the worse for you."

He turned on his heel and was about to leave when Sir Henry stalled him with, "Wait. Wait and tarry awhile. If we are to find this man I need your help. My lands are far-reaching and my men are too few to cover all the ground. Lend me your soldiers so that we can conduct a thorough search."

Sir Thomas was inclined to refuse this request but his need to find Eldroth was more pressing. "I'll send my Captain presently," was the terse response.

When he left, Henry smiled to himself. So far, so good. He would ensure that one of the soldiers was present when Helvin Bog was searched. After that it would be a case of establishing the cause of death with the aid of Father Peter so that no blame was attached to anyone in the manor. Tom Lawkland's deception may just pay off.

***

"Over here, Sir!" cried the potter's apprentice to a soldier. "I think I can see something, someone, in that mire."

The soldier brushed him aside, eager to be the one to get the credit for finding the corpse.

"Careful, Sir, it is treacherous. We must get help," shouted the apprentice boy to the soldier's back.

"My pole is all I need to fish the bastard out," was the reply, while he hooked the halberd end into the dead body's jerkin. "Here, young fellow, help me pull him out."

With a horrid sucking sound the bog released from its grip the cadaver that was Eldroth, the right arm sticking out at a grotesque angle. Mud and slime trickled down the corpse's features as the soldier turned him over on to his front, once he was safely on the bank. The soldier inwardly smiled as he took in the weasel-like features and the lop-sided mouth. He was not sad to see his demise, as Eldroth was well known as a tormentor of the common soldiery. The untouchable one with the King's protection. Now he was dead he could do no one any harm and maybe some good would come of it for the keen-eyed soldier who had found him.

"Quick, go and get the Captain!" barked the soldier at the young apprentice boy. "Tell him that Eldroth has been found dead in the mire. We will need a litter and a horse to take him back. And mind," he said, throwing him a greasy coin, "I was the one that found the bastard, right?"

Within the hour the Captain, two soldiers and the horse-drawn litter had arrived. News of the discovery had spread fast and a horn had summonsed all from far and wide as the search was called off. Sir Henry sent a messenger to beckon Father Peter to establish the cause of death and to say a mass for the soul. The priest duly arrived, astride his mule, his calm bearing immediately halting all the loud gossip and speculation as to what had befallen the corpse.

Sir Thomas immediately tried to take control with a, "Now look here, Father, you must…" but his sentence was cut off with a raised palm of the hand from Father Peter.

"Please, in the name of He who died on the cross, let me have some space. If I am to do my duty properly, let me have time on the matter."

He turned his tonsured head and let his twinkling blue eyes fall on Sir Henry.

"My Lord," he entreated, "can we take this poor departed soul to your hall, where I can wash the corpse and carry out my examination in appropriate surroundings?"

Sir Henry nodded his acquiescence and the litter was taken to the hall where the body was placed on a large trestle table in one of the winter store rooms. Father Peter diligently washed the body as one would a newborn baby. Sir Thomas Courtenay watched the proceedings with growing impatience. In a calm, professional manner the priest examined Eldroth from limb to limb, humming and hawing at each minor discovery. At long last he looked up from his duty to signal that his task was complete.

Sir Thomas could wait no longer. "Well?" he demanded.

"My Lord, this man was a soldier, judging by the many wounds on his person," intoned the priest.

"Goddamn, I know that much," seethed Sir Thomas, forgetting himself.

Father Peter raised his eyebrows at the blasphemy and mildly continued, "But the wounds are old ones and well healed. The man was clearly intoxicated when he fell in Helvin Bog. His hand contains a flagon of wine," and at this he broke the fingers clasped round the wineskin, demonstrating incredible strength, "and nearly an empty flagon of wine at that. He must have been deep in his cups."

Sir Thomas winced at the cracking sound of the priest breaking Eldroth's fingers so matter of factly. "So you are saying there was no foul play?"

"Not a mark on him, and look, you can see here, this bloating of the face is caused by the lungs taking in all the foul water, bringing on death by asphyxiation. Let this be a lesson to all. Intemperance is a sin, punishable by the Almighty. My Lord God is a just God," he concluded as he reached out for a shroud to cover the mortal remains of Eldroth, the sinner.

The soldiery, sinners to a man, looked down at their feet at this holy outburst, and involuntarily began to shuffle out of the room.

"I don't know about you filthy whoresons," said the Captain when they were safely out of earshot, "but this sinner has got the devil's thirst in him that can only be slaked by good honest English ale!"

CHAPTER 12

FRIDAYTHORPE, THE YORKSHIRE WOLDS

But two miles more, and then we rest!
Well, there is still an hour of day,
And long the brightness of the West
Will light us on our devious way;
Sit then, awhile, here in this wood--
So total is the solitude,
We safely may delay.

These massive roots afford a seat,
Which seems for weary travellers made.
There rest. The air is soft and sweet
In this sequestered forest glade,
And there are scents of flowers around,
The evening dew draws from the ground;
How soothingly they spread!

Charlotte Bronte

"THERE IS LITTLE POINT YOU TRAVELLING WITH US," said Tom Lawkland to the two mounted archers, Sir Henry's men assigned to travel with the little group for their protection. "It makes us look like we have something worth stealing or something to hide. Rather stay back but keep us in your sights. If we have need of you, I will sound my horn," he said, patting the giant ram's horn strapped to his belt.

"By my reckoning, we should keep off the main paths afore we turn west

53

for the Dales. I've nivver been to Cumberland afore but I've seen it many a time from Whernside. I reckon if we head for Ripon we can take Mastiles Lane[13] and then get clear on to the estates owned by Fountains Abbey up there. Even if there's a hue and a cry when they find that mangy cattle drover-cum-spy, we'll be long gone. If any o' folk question us on our way, we can allus say we're sheep workers for the Abbey."

The archers saw wisdom in what Tom was saying and nodded their consent. They could halt a small search party but were powerless to stop a concerted effort from the King. At least they had the horsepower to make good their escape if things became too perilous.

Just north of the village of Fridaythorpe, Tom instinctively set his mind's compass west, leading his small party across a cow pasture, the bovine hosts staring wide-eyed at them as they traversed their path. It was all rutted and hard going underfoot, churned up by the cattle, the antithesis of the smooth grazed sheep pastures of the Dales. Before long, they were through this and walking through a sweet meadow, buttercups catching the sun and sawflies hovering like guardian sentinels over this unspoiled patch.

The hills in the distance were now visible. Only small ones, the first bump of the Pennines, but Tom took comfort from the familiar landscape. He would feel a lot safer on home ground, away from these wide open spaces where a mounted soldier could run them down with ease.

The thought minded him of his escort and he checked for the archers over his shoulder, two dots on the horizon. Let's hope their prowess with a bow would not need to be put to good use, he thought.

The immediate fear of capture had left the exiled group as they began to take pleasure in the warm spring sunshine. The boys fanned out, chasing butterflies and grasshoppers as they headed ever westward. Only Bess looked weary, her life softened by village living and waiting attendance on a fine lady. Her travelling clothes were cast-offs from Lady Margaret, when new fashions had taken her fancy, and this gave Bess the appearance of someone of higher rank, set apart from the rest of the rustic-looking ramblers.

"I know it's hard on you," soothed Tom, "but tha'll not get blisters in them fine calf leather boots and afore tha' knows it tha'll be as fit as a lop.[14]

---

13. Mastiles Lane was once part of an important long-distance monastic route.

14. Yorkshire dialect for flea.

In a few days now tha'll be racing lads up yon fells."

Bess tried a weak smile; this was going to be a harrowing journey for her. For someone lowborn, she had had a privileged life. Now there was the prospect of a long journey by foot, open to the elements and the possibility of pursuit by the King's hateful men. She wished she was back in the safety of the castle, somewhere where she could share her thoughts with her own sex, away from this harsh masculine world, where the very sights, sounds and smells were a reminder of the sometime cruelty of Mother Nature. Not so Tom, who strolled on relentlessly, confident of his own ability and the rightfulness of his cause. Let someone get in his way if they dare.

That night the group camped in a copse and Tom lit a fire in a deep hollow, their whereabouts concealed by this and the density of the undergrowth. Not so the two archers whose campfire was visible on the open, sloping ground. Fieldcraft was not their strongpoint, Tom mused, but there again, they had probably no need of concealment when they had been encamped within an army.

Tired of their travel rations, Tom went in search of fresher fare. He set snares for rabbits but that would not yield anything until morning. He set the two younger boys off gathering wild garlic and dandelion leaves for a salad whilst Ralph and he took a sack and went prodding about the undergrowth with their staffs. They soon found what they wanted – hedgehogs snuffling about in the undergrowth – and tallied a couple of brace of the curled up spiny creatures in the sack.

Bess turned her nose up in disgust as Tom covered the creatures in clay and rolled them into the hottest embers of the fire. "You can't expect me to eat that, Husband?" she pleaded.

Tom chuckled and replied, "Tha'll eat 'owt if tha's hungry enough. Besides, this is a tasty enough meal; I've eaten worse fare in my time."

When the meal was ready, the flesh of the hedgehog emitting the rich juicy aroma of pork, literally the hog it was named after, Bess could not resist and had to admit it was succulent and well complemented by the salad leaves.

The boys were ravenous too and Tom let them eat their fill, leaving only the bones for him to chew on. He was used to going without and would compensate for his meagre meal with the rabbits that would be waiting in the snares in the morning.

The next morning he summoned the two archers and they joined the group, greedily tucking in to the fresh spit-roasted rabbits.

"Not much point in your protection from now on. We're way off Sir Henry's land and the lad's mother will be fretting for news of him. Tell her he's safe and well and has the appetite of a young wolf cub. I'd rather keep him for a week than a fortnight." This said as young Henry ate his third saddle of rabbit.

"Nidderdale will soon be in sight and once we're there I'll be able to deal with things on my own terms. Hark on now; I'm grateful to you lads for putting yoursens at risk for me and the lad. If tha'd known the boy's father, tha'd know that he was worth it."

The archers took their leave, grateful that their brief affair with danger was over. These were troubled times and many a man was in a quandary to declare where his true loyalty lay, whether it be to the new King Edward, the old King Henry or just to his hearth and home. God damn this civil strife.

CHAPTER 13

THOMAS LAWKLAND - THE OLD ROMAN CAMP, MASTILES LANE, MALHAMDALE

IT WAS WHEN WE WERE HEADING FOR Joss Hawkshaw's place that I began to see the lad come alive. Joss was one of my old shepherds when I was Reeve to Lord John. A typical Dalesman of the old kind, dark as you like, with tawny eyes that didn't miss a trick.

We'd travelled far and you couldn't blame anyone for being weary, but not so our Moses, Henry that was. Nineteen questions to the dozen about what creature this was and why was that tree growing sideways out of the hill. He'd instantly changed from a quiet, taciturn young chap into a chattering magpie. And I suppose the Dales are a magical place. Well, they are to me, anyroad; it's just that I'd not seen them fresh through the eyes of a young lad, for the first time like.

Why, we'd passed through becks stained brown with ironstone and others that disappeared under ground one minute only to turn up again a mile downstream. And by each one, pied and yellow wagtails with their tails seesawing on the water's edge. Each one wi' a mouthful of flies.

He couldn't take his eyes off the peregrine falcons wheeling overhead, their young 'uns mewing to be fed, tucked up in the limestone crag. And when you looked up, clouds were scudding across the sky and leaving big racing shadows on t'other side o' the fell.

Then, the wind came soughing through ash trees on slopes o' the valley and I looked up to see a storm brewing. I got them all under me old waxed sail cloth to keep 'em dry while weather passed, and I sat outside by the drystone wall for shelter, watching 'em like. When the hailstones hit them, big as goose

57

eggs, there was such a hullabaloo within, laughing and screaming and the tent moving this way and that like some big floundering animal. Afore long they were singing songs from the nursery, and chanting out old words for sheep counting. Yan, tan, tether! Like some ancient battle cry. I think they were disappointed when it stopped for they asked when there'd be another.

The limestone pavement was tricky after that, covered in an icy, greasy film that made you slip every third step. Moses was still on his journey of exploration, looking a'tween the cracks at purple flowers and hart's ferns. And beyond that a carpet of smooth velvet green grass.

"Stay close, our Moses, we don't want you twisting your ankle," Bess pleaded, drawing him in close to her. And then he just came out with it.

"Are we in heaven, Mother?"

She stopped, in a state of shock, then pulled him closer, tears welling in her eyes at this sign of familial affection.

"No, we are high up in the world but we're a long way from heaven yet," she gulped, swallowing her tears whilst smiling at him.

"Who made all this?" he asked.

"Why, God made this of course," was the response.

"Well, we must be in heaven then, silly Mother," he said, smiling at her and giving her protective arm a playful nudge.

My Bess looked at me entreatingly. I nodded. An exchange of words was not needed.

Then he saw two of Joss' dogs slinking down the path with lolling tongues and mischievous eyes, like wolves, watchful and knowing. He beckoned them and they came running, jumping up to greet him and circling round, their tails wagging like great black and white plumes. Ralph and Luke were a bit more wary at first but soon made friends and went scampering off with the dogs to find their master.

Joss nodded.

"Maister, tha'll be wanting some lodgings for the night," as if he had only seen me yesterday. He must have known about the hue and cry around the countryside regarding our whereabouts but made no immediate acknowledgement of this. As I say, he was a typical taciturn Dalesman. His wife made a fuss of Bess who was only too relieved to have a roof over her head.

Just like old times, Joss took me round to inspect the flock, this time with the boys in tow, pointing out this tup[15] or that yaw,[16] and commenting on the quality of the pasture. He smiled as he showed the boys the cave where the troglodyte sheep lived, to shelter from some of the worst winter weather. They didn't believe him at first but when stalwart Ralph, the first to explore, ran out with a tup butting at his heels, they burst out in gales of laughter.

"So that's Lord Clifford's eldest," mused Joss.

I was right, he did know our predicament.

"That's our Moses now," I corrected him gently.

"Well I'll tell thee summat, Maister," observed Joss. "That lad's smitten with thee. Look how he's resting on his crook just the same way that tha' does. He watches your every move and makes to mimic you. And has tha' seen how he 'as a way wi' dogs? Tha's got a first-rate shepherd on thy 'ands there, and make no mistake."

As before, there was no need for further words.

Joss' place was on the old Roman Camp atop o' Mastiles Lane. As we climbed the fell to go home for supper the grouse scuttled through the heather with their haunting cry of "go back, go back, go back".

"Go back, yoursen," called Moses, picking up the native tongue. I ruffled Moses' hair and called to the lads, "Sixpence for the first one home," as I watched them leaping and wading through the heather.

"I'm first!" shouted Ralph, "the sixpence is mine!"

"Nay, that dog there beat thee by two lengths," I laughed when I reached the shepherd's dwelling.

The boys piled into me with their little fists flailing. "Tha's a big twister. Tha' said nowt about dogs." I carried the two younger ones under my arms and dropped them on the doorstep.

"Now mind your manners, lads, or there'll be no supper for you and it's bed on an empty stomach."

The smell of the rich mutton stew and fresh baked bread ensured their integrity and they looked greedily at the steaming bowls put down before them by Joss' wife and Bess.

Joss held the boys in thrall with tall tales of giants, hobgoblins and fairy

---

15. A ram.
16. A ewe.

folk hiding behind every stone, and in the candlelight their eyes grew large as saucers.

"That's enough excitement for one night," scolded their mother. "Time for all good boys to pray to baby Jesus and get straight to sleep."

The next morning, throwing caution and all sense of urgency to the wind, I decided to take Moses on a little detour, showing him some of the wonders this miraculous Dale had to offer. I woke him just before dawn and with a hushing motion, whispered in his ear:

> *"Little Boy Blue, come blow your horn,*
> *The sheep's in the meadow, the cow's in the corn.*
> *Where is the boy who looks after the sheep?*
> *He's under a haycock, fast asleep.*
> *Will you wake him?*
> *No, not I,*
> *For if I do, he's sure to cry."*

Traditional nursery rhyme, Anon

He smiled conspiratorially at me, and we tiptoed past the rest of the sleeping, exhausted bodies. It would do Bess a power of good to rest for a day, I justified to myself.

I led him down to Gordale Scar, stepping lightly through the rivulets of water as we approached the cliff edge that obscured the view from afar. When we turned the corner and saw the spouting waterfalls in all their glory, his mouth gaped open. One waterfall juxtaposed after another as the black racing waters crashed downwards, the whole thing reaching upwards to the heavens. The noise was like thunder and I could just make out his voice in the deafening roar.

"Does the devil live here, or one of the demons that Joss was telling us about?"

"Not that I know of. Would you like to climb it to find out?" I ventured.

He looked unsure.

"I've climbed it afore, tha' knows, and I'm still here to tell the tale."

This time he nodded and I took his hand to guide him up the treacherous, slippery path, sometimes immersed in the cold icy water, sometimes slithering on the rocky path. Upwards and upwards with the crags seeping water out of their sides and the roaring waterfall in our ears.

When we reached the top I asked, "Happy now?" and he laughed. He laughed like a lad with not a care in the world. The laugh of someone who'd climbed one of the highest peaks and who'd come out the other end unscathed.

We came back down a different route on one of the many screes that lined the fells. The opposite side, with limestone jutting out from the mountainside, caught the morning sun and took on the appearance of a giant's ribcage protruding from the earth. No wonder Joss said giants lived here.

Janet's Foss was where I used to dip the sheep before shearing. We weaved our way through a path of twisted roots and greasy stones in a wooded limestone valley. The edges were carpeted with wild garlic, Herb Paris, Dog's Mercury and Lords-and-Ladies. You could hear the roar of the tiny waterfall before you saw it but nonetheless the sight was spectacular as the waters tumbled into a great natural pool.

"I learned to swim in there," I blurted, wishing I had not, for this was followed with a pleading of, "Will you teach me?"

"Maybe not today, 'cause we haven't got that much time, but happen another day."

The disappointment on his face was all too plain to see.

"This is Janet's Foss or Jennet's Foss, the fairy queen that Joss was telling thee about. I've never seen her like, but some folk swears as they's seen her many a time."

"Can we see her today?" entreated Moses.

"Well, it's not just a case of seeing her," I stalled, "she appears to you when she wants to be seen."

His look showed that he did not believe me.

"But I tell you what I do," I continued. He nodded for me to go on.

"Well, mark the sun that shines atop those branches."

He nodded again.

"Well, screw your eyes up real tight. What you're looking for is a golden haze and when you see that you stare straight into it. Then close your eyes and open them again, and if she's in a mind – only if she's in a mind, mark thee – then she'll appear to thee. Dost tha' think tha' can do that?" He solemnly nodded his assent and turned his face to the golden orb of the morning sun.

"I can see her, I can see her, Tom!" he squealed.

"Oh, it's Tom now, is it?" I chuckled, trying to sound stern.

"Fatha, then!" he cried, still in a high state of excitement.

"Fatha," I winked. He tried to wink back at me with a lop-sided blinking of his eyes. I laughed and he laughed back.

That was one of many special times we had together. Just the two of us. Father and son.

CHAPTER 14

SKIPTON CASTLE

THE HERALD, RESPLENDENT IN THE LIVERY OF the Stanleys, announced the arrival of Sir William Stanley.

"Let it be known to one and all that the Right Honourable and mine especial good Lord, Sir William Stanley, right humble and wise, is proclaimed Lord of Skipton Castle and all the Craven manors, by his Royal Majesty King Edward IV. This scion of the House of York recommends him to you as one of his most valuable jewels and bids that you do your duty in giving attendance on him as it were for a prince. And you shall find him so reasonable that you shall of reason be content and he shall be so disposed to you."

The audience in the main hall was sparse and inattentive. They lined up against the wall hangings, shuffling their feet and staring at the far wall.

Sir William made his grand entrance with a large retinue of followers, all of whom were almost entirely dressed in black, all the more to show off his gaudy purple and white quartered doublet. He was of middling height with a large protruding belly and bulbous nose set in a face the colour of a rooster's wattle. His shoulder-length hair was fair and thinning and combed over the top of his pate to cover his baldness.

He looked about him, deflated and clearly disappointed to see such a meagre household staff. It immediately put him in a bad humour. He singled out one of the oldest servants, more plainly dressed than the rest, with bandy legs that defied him staying upright.

"You there! Come hither. What is your name?" he barked.

The old fellow doffed his cap, fingering it round the rim, and crabbed his way forward.

"Gasper, Sir," he mumbled.

"Gasper, what sort of heathen name is that?" he asked in an imperious tone.

"Don't know, Sir, it's just a name as I've allus had. Some folks say me proper name's Caspar but Gasper has allus suited me fine," he replied in a wheezing voice that set him off in to a hacking cough. "Farmer's lung, Sir," he said by way of explanation, adding a toothless smile.

"Well, farmer Gasper, what is your duty round here? Oh, and when you address me, you address me as My Lord," he said in a loud resonant pitch, for the benefit of the rest of the household staff.

"Shepherd's Reeve, Sir; I mean, Shepherd's Reeve, milord," he corrected himself, looking up from beetling black eyebrows.

The rest of the staff looked on to see how this was playing out, lest the same interrogation befell them.

"And how is the state of your flocks, Master Gasper? I understand that wool is to be a staple of my income here."

"Oh terrible, Sir, I means, milord. What with the worst winter in living memory and the war with the thieving soldier scum stealing from under our noses we have but half what we should 'ave," he sputtered in his rattling voice.

"Well look here," Sir William puffed, "it's just not good enough, see? I want to see your tally immediately, do you understand me?"

"Tally, Sir?" enquired Gasper.

"Yes, tally, records, ledgers. Go and get them," said a clearly irritated Sir William.

"Can't, Sir," was the terse reply.

"'Can't sir?' I mean My Lord. I thought I told you to call me my Lord!" he shouted. "Why can't you get them?"

Gasper looked up. He had everyone's attention now. After a lengthy pause he ventured, "Can't, Sir, 'cause I have neither the reading nor the writing so it would be no good to the likes o' me."

The assembled staff stifled a giggle.

Sir William turned puce and bellowed, "Can't read or write? What sort of a household is this? I suppose the cooks don't know how to make a broth? And I thought I told you to call me My Lord!" he enunciated in a staccato fashion.

"Yes, Sir," said Gasper, looking sideways at the staff.

This time the giggles were not suppressed and some of Sir Stanley's own retinue let out a guffaw.

Sir William exploded. "Have you never served a Lord before? What is this pitiful excuse of a retinue I see before me? Surely Lady Margaret would not have tolerated this? I had a mind to make her a marriage offer but now I am not entirely sure of my reason. Have you people no manners?"

"Ain't been much call for it afore, Sir, I means Your Worship. Lord John never had much time for fancy manners and bowing and scraping and that. Said that stuff could be saved for when the King came to visit as long as we got on with our duties," Gasper explained in his crackling, rasping voice.

"Get out!" stuttered Sir William.

"Beg your pardon, Sir?" enquired Gasper, cupping his hand over his ear.

"Get out now. Out of my sight. You're dismissed from office. I'll bring in some proper shepherds from my Cheshire estates. And get out the rest of you. I've had quite enough for one day. Someone fetch me a cup of malmsey," he ordered, turning his livid face to the wall.

Outside in the courtyard, the household body crowded around old Gasper. Oliver Howgill, the Airedale bailiff said, "Well old fellow, you've talked yourself out of office. If you'd kept a civil tongue in your head, you might have had Master Lawkland's job yet."

"Why that silly old fool," said Gasper, taking off his cap and combing his lank hair over his head in imitation of Sir William. He raised one leg in the air and broke wind. This was met with hoots of laughter from the assembled staff.

"Marry Lady Margaret? Why that fat bastard hasn't seen his own codpiece in the last twenty years. He's worth nowt."

"That's as maybe," remarked Oliver Howgill, "but he's a nowt that's cost you your livelihood."

"Cost me my livelihood? Me? Come on, Davey," he motioned towards a red-haired young lad, "we've work to do. Get your cloak."

"Where are we going, Gasper?" asked the boy.

"Why, we're going to take milord's flock up to me nephew's pasture on Swaledale. That silly old bugger doesn't know a tup from a yaw. It would be downright daft not to take such a present from under the nose of a high and mighty peer of the realm," he cackled.

CHAPTER 15

WESTMORLAND

THEY MADE AN ODD SPECTACLE, THE LITTLE group of travellers travers-
ing the moorland and mountain paths.

The shepherd and his three boys were nut brown and weather-
beaten from the sun and elements, clearly comfortable striding across the
hills. The woman, dressed like a fine lady, had shied away from the sun
and covered her head with the hood of her travelling cloak. She struggled
to make the pace that the others had set but they were patient and there
was no hurry.

Thomas and Bess had argued about the best way to go about their
journey, for she was tired and longed to sleep on a proper mattress with
a roof over her head. A wayside inn would do. She could play the part
of a lady, accompanied by her household's manservant and his boys en
route to Yanwath Hall. Thomas had argued for caution and felt safer on
familiar terrain, rather than expose themselves to questions and stares
in a crowded noisy inn. He was adept at living out of doors and made a
comfortable enough shelter and bed out of ling[17]. Even though this was
his first time in Westmorland he was the sort of man who could naturally
read the countryside, instinctively spotting the best places to rest and
hunt and forage for food. There was the odd shepherd's shelter up on
the shielings[18] and occasionally they would meet other shepherds who
offered hospitality.

Why hurry to a destination where all they would be doing was mark-
ing time until it was safe to make a reappearance? Better to take in the
cottongrass, the harebells and the lapwings wheeling overhead, the fierce

17. Heather.
18. Temporary building or pasture.

eagle on its mountain eyrie and the peregrine falcons dropping out of the sky like a stone, to clutch savagely at the migrant birds newly arrived for spring.

After a day or two, though, he started to feel uneasy, like he was being watched or followed. Was it his paranoia or was there someone really there? Someone in pursuit, likely to do them harm, or someone spying on them? If it were the case, then the latter was to be the more likely as anyone in pursuit would have made their move by now.

If there was someone there, he or she were good, as they had not disturbed any of the wildlife or left any signs of intrusion. But it was there, that nagging at the back of his brain, a sixth sense or survival instinct or what you will. It made him angry and determined to surprise the perpetrator before they were surprised themselves. He had to get the upper hand in this situation.

He thought long and hard about the puzzle. He was convinced that someone's eyes were watching him, but, without seeing any signs, how was he to make his move? At length, he struck upon the solution. If his keen shepherd's eyes could not see anything it was because there was nothing to see, at least where he was looking. He was just looking in the wrong place. If he searched for signs behind his back, on the trail follow- ing them, then that may be a different proposition.

That evening, he saw the signal he'd been searching for. On the side of the fell, to the left, a family of grouse took off as if startled by some- thing. There were some large boulders, big enough to conceal a man, on that side. Their pursuer was there all right. He decided to make camp there and then and found a shelter in the lee of the hill, in full view of the boulders opposite. He tasked the boys with gathering ling to build a makeshift shelter whilst he lit a fire so that Bess could make the evening meal, all the time looking in the direction of the boulders.

"What's amiss?" asked Bess anxiously; "you look distracted."

"Nothing, my love," was Tom's distant response. "Just admiring the view."

By dawn the following morning, Tom had positioned himself atop the hill, moving through the night as silently as a cat. The valley below was shrouded with mist, the tips of the boulders just showing through the low cloud. As the sun's rays became stronger the vapour slowly burnt off, exposing the boulders, great erratics that were remnants of the ice age. They looked like they'd been placed there by giants.

Tom sat watching patiently. Soon he got what he was waiting for. Almost directly below him was a slumbering figure, a man, in the lee of the largest of the lichen-covered rocks. He drew in a deep breath and then hurled himself down the scree at breakneck pace, covering the descent in a few seconds. The man, aroused by the sudden noise and small avalanche of rocks, started and looked up at the shocking apparition of Tom, framed in view by the bright yellow sunlight like some avenging angel. He tried to raise himself up and reach for his sword at the same time but his limbs were stiff from sleep and the cold morning air, his cloak tangling in his right arm. He did not even make it to his feet when Tom, using the momentum of his descent, rammed his staff into the man's solar plexus. He expelled a great welt of air and clutched at his abdomen.

Tom pulled him roughly to his feet and placed his flensing knife across the gasping man's throat. He took in the bright red jupon that gave his captive's identity away as a soldier. He was a barrel-chested, powerful-looking man of middling height with a very dark complexion, a blue-black growth of whiskers on his chin.

"Right, talk. Speak, tell me who you are and who you serve. Who sent you here? Tell me or I'll slit your evil-looking throat!" Tom said through gritted teeth, the struggle of containing his victim taking all his strength and concentration. He pricked the fellow's chin with the point of his knife.

"Amis, friends," spluttered the soldier. "You and I, we are both the fugitif. I am the soldat of Burgougne. Je me suis échappé de la bataille chez Towton. Je suis venu ici avec les soldats écossais mais ils m'ont laissé."

This response momentarily threw Tom off his stride and he tightened his grip on the soldier's jupon with his left hand. The man winced in pain and Tom felt the struggle go out of him.

"Blessé, how you say? A wound," explained the man. Tom, not quite knowing what to do next, took two steps backwards and motioned for the soldier to remove his jupon. When he did so, he revealed an angry looking wound that had refused to knit and was secreting pus.

Tom knelt down to collect the man's cloak and sword, keeping his eyes on him all the time. He prodded him with his staff and nodded down to the encampment where Bess and the children were just stirring. The man complied meekly enough and set off across the valley floor in a strange ambling gait.

Their entrance at the Lawkland camp caused quite a commotion. The boys ran to greet them but Bess shrieked for them to come back and clasped the two younger ones close to her.

"We have got ourselves a visitor," said Tom, throwing the captured sword to Ralph. "If he makes so much as a move, run him through with this."

Bess's eyes expressed a look of horror and then concern as she took in the wound on the man's right shoulder. "That needs treating right away," she said firmly.

Tom rolled his eyes and barked at Luke and Moses. "Right, you two, get thasens to the stand o' them birch trees. Tha's looking for comfrey. Tha' knows what that looks like Luke, doesn't tha'?"

Luke nodded and the two wide-eyed boys headed for the woodland, all the time looking over their shoulder at the new arrival.

While they were foraging for the comfrey, or wound wort as it was known locally, Bess tried her best to communicate with the wounded soldier whilst Ralph stood guard, trying to look fierce with his new sword, and Tom looked dispassionately on.

Bess had picked up some Court French whilst serving with Lady Margaret but the man's Burgundian French was quite a distinct and different dialect to her Norman French and initially proved to be a challenge. From what she could make out, his name was Gaston and he was part of the Burgundian mercenaries that had been engaged by Margaret of Anjou to swell the Lancastrian forces. He had been enlisted for good wages and promised plunder when the Lancastrian troops moved southwards, with the hope of pillaging the rich farmsteads of the southern shires. Instead, he had received nothing but hardship and, routed at Towton, made good his escape with a small band of Scottish mercenaries homeward bound on this less obvious western route. His wound was debilitating, though, and he could not keep up with the rest, so they had left him behind with a small provision of food.

He was watching their group with interest and had come to the opinion that they were refugees from the recent turmoil, just like him. He had decided to present himself that morning when he had been so rudely awoken by Tom. At this he mimicked the big wild figure of Tom, standing on his toes to look taller and screwing his face up to make a brutal countenance.

Tom spat sideways at the turf. "He's lying. He's been following us for days. How do we know he can't speak proper English instead o' blathering like an ape? I might just as well slit his throat now and have done wi' it."

"You'll do no such thing!" cried Bess. "This is a Christian land and we're Christian people. Shame on you. There's been too much bloodshed already. This poor soul is half starved to death and if he doesn't get this wound treated he'll die. I want you to show him some compassion."

Gaston did not understand the words but, looking at Tom's grumbling expression, he understood the sentiment. He grovelled at Bess's feet and kissed the hem of her kirtle with a "Bénissez-vous, madame".

Tom growled his acquiescence and Gaston, slowly rising, gave him a sheepish smile and finished off the encounter with a Gallic shrug.

"Aye, and I'll be watching thee, tha' French bugger!" said Tom with a flinty stare.

Luke and Moses returned with armfuls of young comfrey leaves. Bess washed the wound, Gaston wincing all the while, and Tom applied the green hairy leaves to the wound with a bit more force than perhaps was needed. He then bound the area with linen, wrapping it around the shoulder. Gaston replaced his soldier's jupon and wriggled at the discomfort caused by the rough texture of the leaves.

Bess soothed him with a, "C'est normale. La manière de la nature."

After breakfast, at which Gaston ate heartily, Tom was keen that they break camp and make as many miles as possible that day. When all their gear was packed Tom said firmly to Bess, "If yon fellow's travelling with us I want his hands binding. I don't trust 'im. He'd cut your throat soon as look at you. And I'm not being harsh, he's a mercenary, remember?

I've you and the lads to think of. Tell him he's got to be bound."

Bess looked apologetically at Gaston and said, "Vous faites comme le prisonnier de guerre," holding her upturned wrists forward. Gaston shot a sly look at Tom, emitted another Gallic shrug, and held his hands out to be bound.

Tom wound the leather cord around his wrists tight, with a tug at each completed rotation, all the while looking Gaston firmly in the eye.

"That's right, you and I understand each other, my mucker. Try 'owt on and I'll ram your sword so far up your arse it'll come out of your chops."

Bess tut-tutted and scolded Tom for using such language in front of the children whilst Ralph turned sideways to stifle his laughter.

CHAPTER 16

SWALEDALE

Go, lowly Swale: go headlong down,
Down through your stony-faced meadows,
Your scowling hills, your crouching towns.
Go, little Swale, and I follow.

The taciturn hill farmers patiently still
Are pacing their hillside;
The po-faced sheep stare as they go.
The pinafored women go day after day
Making their hay
Down by the river edge where wagtails are trotting,
By Booze, by Muker, by Gunnerside, by Crackpot.

Go, little Swale: go headlong down,
Down through your stony-faced meadows,
Your scowling hills, your crouching towns.
Go, little Swale, and I follow.

Jake Thackray
© Leola Music Limited

SWALEDALE IS THE NORTHERNMOST OF THE YORKSHIRE Dales and so remote that it's as good a place as any to hide something as conspicuous as several large flocks of sheep. Its steep-sided slopes descend into lush green valleys, chequered with dry stone walls. The glinting mountain streams spill down into the River Swale, England's fastest flowing river, which careers through a smattering of small villages whose names betray their Norse origins.

Lord Stanley's prize ram looked down the fells on Gunnerside with utter content and appraised the lush pasture and healthy ewes. His lambs were fat and plentiful. This was a good place to live for a sheep.

Down in the valley, Gasper had tears in his eyes when he explained to his nephew how he'd duped the mighty Lord Stanley. Tears of laughter. Encouraged by young Davey, he repeated the tale of how this pretentious man had tried to impose his authority on his new charges. He hadn't realized that these people had a strong independent streak and that even wars and famine had not bowed them. Respect had to be earned and any sign of weakness was ruthlessly exploited.

"And he says to me, 'go get your tally'. 'Can't Sir,' says I. 'You mean milord,' says he. 'Why can't you get the tally?' 'Cause I can't read or write Sir,' says I," Gasper wheezed. "Me that's stood on the shire jury for nigh on twenty year and can write better than a scribe."

The three men surrendered themselves to another fit of unrestrained laughter.

"And all the while he's huffing and puffing and blustering and milording and I'm takkin' all his best flock up here and leaving him the old drafted ewes whose teeth are too old to chew the heather. Tally my arse. Tom Lawkland knew every lamb that were born across thirty manors. Tha'd get nowt past 'im. And I'll tell thee summat else. I've not finished wi' that fat peacock milord Stanley. There's more sport and more money to be had yet."

"What may that be, uncle?" asked his incredulous nephew.

"Why, I'll fatten these sheep up on these high pastures, out of the way here for a season. Milord Stanley will like as not get someone from his Cheshire estates to look after what's left of his flock and strengthen their numbers with some longwool sheep from thereabouts. They'll not last two months into the winter. The foraging will be too sparse for some of them and the cold will kill the rest off.

"And, when he's wringing his hands and mourning his losses, I'll poll up there and sell him his old sheep back and charge him a King's ransom for his best tup."

"Nay, tha'd not dare, Uncle," marvelled the nephew.

"Just you watch 'im," cut in young Davey, and the trio fell into fits of stomach wrenching laughter again.

The duping of William Stanley was all the more poignant as he and his elder brother, Thomas, were appointed by Edward IV to set up a commission on wool exports. Their duty was to enquire into the whereabouts of wool and hides that were in various ports in England instead of Calais, thus depriving the King of export revenue. No doubt some of Gasper's new fleeces were among them.

This appointment was greeted with much mirth by the north country folk and only served to ridicule Lord Stanley further. He was a thick-skinned creature, though, and he and his family had a shameful record in warfare. His elder brother, Lord Thomas Stanley, had mobilised a large number of Cheshire men for the first battle at St Albans but conveniently arrived too late to commit to either side. He waited on the turn of events, later commenting that they regretted not having arrived at the battle in time to fight, and hoped that they could be of service at a later time.

The family, having avoided being directly involved in the battle of St Albans, moved deftly from the Lancastrian cause to the House of York when it came into the ascendancy, without any shame or remorse. They were determined to keep the power, position and lands they inherited and played the political game with canny astuteness in a time of great uncertainty.

William Stanley had all the hallmarks of his family and greedily held on to Skipton Castle. It bothered him not that the people did not show him respect or affection, like they had for the Cliffords. As long as he had money in his purse he cared not for the opinions or feeling of others.

He had not acquired vast wealth by being a total fool and was the sort that would bide his time to gain revenge. That applied to the likes of old Gasper and anyone else that stood in his path, low-born or noble.

CHAPTER 17

YANWATH HALL, CUMBERLAND

THE WEATHER WAS FOUL. THE RAIN HAD been grisling, as Tom called it, for two days now. The poor visibility had not helped their journey and Tom, who prided himself on his sense of direction, had to ask for guidance from a farmer, weeding his crop of oats on the terraced valley sides.

Now that they were nearing their destination, the small group of travellers were somewhat deflated; all their energy had been spent getting here and having so very nearly achieved their objective, they let out a collective sigh and contemplated what might be in store for them. Tom was particularly weary. He had been powered by an enormous adrenalin rush these past few weeks and now that the immediate danger was over his body tripped into a sluggardly recovery mode.

Soon, though, the sun threatened to break through the livid edge of the cloud and before long they were squinting ahead into bright sunshine. The harsh landscape became gentler and the sun picked out the relief of the dragon-back hills, crested with dry stone walls like some mighty slumbering reptile.

Yanwath Hall comprised a solid square fortified tower abutted by a manor house. A stone coat of arms was carved into a tablet above the studded door, a red cross on a silver shield, denoting the arms of Sir Lancelot Threlkeld.

The dogs heralded their arrival and Sir Lancelot himself pushed past the soldiers to greet his new guests. His eyes ran over the group and rested on young Henry, bedraggled and dressed in rough fustian. He turned to Tom and smiled.

"You have done well." His rich deep-brown voice revealed a slight hint of a Cumbrian accent.

Tom liked him all the more for this and returned the smile. He bowed and introduced the group.

"This is my good wife, Bess, my eldest lad, Ralph, Luke and our Moses," – the last name said with deep meaning and an open stare at Sir Lancelot.

Bess curtseyed, the boys inclined their heads and Gaston coughed, raised his eyes heavenward and held his bound hands forward.

"Oh, and yon fellow there that looks like an old sheep chewing a turnip, is Gaston, or so he says. We picked the poor beggar up along the way. He reckons he fought at Towton but I didn't trust him none so I bound his hands."

Sir Lancelot broke into a flurry of French in a heavily accented, staccato English way, and soon Gaston was nodding, shrugging and inclining his head this way and that.

Lancelot drew his dagger and cut the bonds, to the relief of Gaston who stood rubbing his chafed wrists.

"What he told you was right enough," said Lancelot. "He's a Burgundian mercenary who fought under the banner of Margaret of Anjou at Towton. He speaks a different dialect to Norman French; that's why you had difficulty in understanding things. His Scottish companions passed through here last week, a right sorry looking lot. I must say that's the first time I've felt sorry for a Scotsman. Anyhow, he's going to be my soldier now. I can always do with a skilled man at arms in these troubled times and he'll help patrol against the thieving Douglas's that raid my sheep and cattle. Allez, Gaston, manger vous."

Gaston looked in Tom's direction and when he had engaged his eye he smiled, shrugged his shoulders and departed with a wink. Tom growled under his breath like some irritable old guard dog.

"Now, let's get you cleaned up and fed and watered and I'll show you where you are staying tonight. I'll explain my plans over dinner. You can dine with me and my steward. He can be trusted, don't worry," confided Sir Lancelot.

That night over dinner, Tom studied Sir Lancelot Threlkeld, who was to be his new master. He was young, in his early twenties, but with a self-assured way that commanded authority. He had fair hair and hazel eyes and was slim, athletic and full of energy. He was passionate about the Lancastrian cause and confided in them that a band of Lancastrian followers had taken refuge just over the border in Scotland. If Tom's position was betrayed and if Edward sent forces northwards for young Clifford's capture, they could soon send word across the border and rally a small army to defend themselves.

Bess paid little heed to this but was delighted when she was told that they were to live at Threlkeld Hall, the ancestral seat of Sir Lancelot. It was a small manor house, not nearly so grand as Yanwath Hall, but nonetheless a substantial property and she would be the chatelaine while Tom would be Lancelot's reeve, responsible for his cattle and numerous flocks of sheep. Tom would give each boy the responsibility of looking after a flock themselves, and no one was more delighted than Moses.

Over the next few days, Tom took stock of their situation. He was back to his old job. On a much smaller estate, granted, but a job he loved doing. He had a fine house to live in and this made his wife happy. The boys were learning a useful occupation and were out of danger's way, if you discounted marauding Scots raiders. The people here were friendly and the dialect was not very different to Yorkshire and he soon had a close affinity with them. Lady Margaret would be able to visit them from time to time without provoking the suspicion of anyone hereabouts who really cared. He felt he could relax and enjoy himself for the first time in months. Sir Lancelot had got himself a good deal. The hardest working reeve in the North and three apprentice shepherds who would help build up his livestock. A French soldier into the bargain too, he chuckled to himself.

"Now then, Moses," said Tom, "tha's thee own master now. Them sheep that's hefted to yon fell are your responsibility."

"Heaved," corrected Moses. "The folk round here say heaved and not hefted like we do in Yorkshire."

"That's as maybe but you're responsible for every bit of fleece on their backs," replied Tom, trying to look serious. He found it hard to suppress the pride he felt for this boy, orphaned and then born again to this humble yet joyful calling.

He was given charge of a flock of over a hundred sheep and was to live up on the shieling with them to get the best out of the summer pastures. He had two collies and a mastiff for his companions, the latter to guard the sheep from predators. Tom didn't doubt that he had the mastery of the dogs for the boy had a way about him with all animals.

"Now, does tha' think tha' can manage it?" asked Tom. "Them beasts is worth a lot of money and I've to account to Sir Lancelot for every single one."

"If I can't look after them, then tha's not taught me very well then, hast tha', Fatha?" replied Moses with a smile.

Tom cuffed him gently on the head and sent him on his way.

"On tha' way, clever Dick," said Tom, "and you mark my words about them Scotsmen. Dogs will let you know if there's anyone abouts, so listen to what they tell thee and get down that fell wi' all the speed tha' can muster."

Tom looked on with satisfaction as Moses picked up his crook, whistled for the dogs and set off for the dark brooding fell. Although still a boy, he was to all intents and purposes a man now, expected to do a man's job. There was to be no mollycoddling him at Threlkeld Hall. That was Lady Margaret's instruction and that suited them all fine. Tom had an extra son and a shepherd to mould in his own image; Moses was out on the fells doing what he so obviously enjoyed and all was good with their world. A tiny corner of peace in a war-ravaged kingdom.

The sheep bleated in the distance. Herdwick sheep, a strange dark grey colour with a white face poking through a frizzy fleece. They were the only breed that could withstand the foul weather of the Lake District, their fleeces repelling all the rain and their hooves withstanding footrot in the dank conditions.

Folk said that these were a breed that were left here by the Vikings. It felt like no one from the outside world had visited here since those times.

CHAPTER 18

THOMAS LAWKLAND, HELVELLYN

MY FATHA HAD A WAY ABOUT HIM with dogs. He used to breed them and everyone wanted a sheepdog from his kennels. The dogs were intelligent, independent yet biddable. He could get them dogs to round up the sheep like no one tha's seen before. No one until our Moses, that is.

The lad's favourite dog was Chad. A dog he'd raised from a pup. The two were inseparable and Moses would not be parted from him, nor Chad from he. It was not surprising really as the two kept each other company during the solitary summer months high up on the fell.

I visited all the boys from time to time as Bess would worry about their safety, but none of my fold was more content than Moses.

One starlit night, sat by the camp fire, he said to me, "I see him, you know, my father, up there in the sky like you told me. You may think me mad but if I screw up my eyes like you taught me at Janet's Foss, I can see his face. He talks to me sometimes too. He helped me find a lamb I'd lost when even Chad couldn't find it. He talks to me when I'm lonely and tells me to be in good spirits. I just wish he was here. Not as a mighty Lord but as a simple shepherd, living with us. Seeing all the beauty around us and sharing a bowl of Mother's mutton stew and laughing at Luke's silly jesting. Rising at dawn's chorus with us to see the rising plants and sniff the cold air.

"He would be happy then. No enemies to fight. No law and punishment to mete out, just here amongst friends and family. I sometimes think he never had a happy life."

"Nay, he did, lad," I said, "for he had thee and tha'd bring joy to anyone's heart. He just had a different way about him than us. Tha' can't be a fine lord like him and then chew on a piece of grass like us and spend your time sitting out under the stars."

"I try and count every one of them," said Moses. "I spend hours looking at them every night when there's a clear sky. They're like familiar friends and I imagine that all them there," he said pointing to the Milky Way, "lead to my father's house."

"Happen they do lad, happen they do," I said.

I often used to watch him while he was unawares, while he was working the dogs or just laid out flat on his back looking at the scudding clouds or more often than not gazing at the stars at night. He used to talk to himsen, but he were really trying to talk to his father. They had a right old natter. He'd pick on a star and ask his father what this one or that one were called and, judging by his reply, you'd swear blind he had got himsen' an answer.

Then, I used to walk up to him gently like, the dogs wagging their tails to greet me, and he'd look up with that great big smile of his and say, "What's to do, Fatha?" He seemed happy enough. If you asked him outright he said he was content and wouldn't swap his place for all the King's jewels.

But it was with the dogs that he came alive. The big fierce mastiff lived with the sheep and took on their scent. He was the lead animal in the flock and no wolves would venture near when he were around. But he were like a big soft puppy around our Moses though, rolling on his back and whimpering and yapping like one of me Lady's lapdogs.

The collies were matchless, though, and Chad the best bar none. He were a grand looking dog, wall-eyed – one eye brown and t'other blue that is – with a long, glossy black and white coat. He had tufts of hair on his ears and a long plume of a tail that steered him like a ship's rudder across the rolling ocean of grass on the fell side.

To see Moses working him were a sight to behold. I don't know if tha's watched a working sheepdog but it's the nearest thing to a wolf tha'll see. Its instinct is to kill sheep. Only thing that prevents it from doing so is that it thinks that tha's the pack leader and so it takes its instructions from you. It naturally crawls on its belly when it approaches sheep so, by the time they see it coming, they're panicked and it can rush them into going in whatever direction it wants. They don't have time to think about where they can run to escape. The dogs can run, half-crouching in that manner too, just like a wolf would so's it can get closer. And when they burst into full speed to get round sheep they run at a fair old lick, easily outpacing fastest o' the sheep. When all's done and you finally pen them all up, it sits there looking at you as pack leader like, saying to itsen, "why doesn't that silly beggar kill 'em and eat 'em then?"

Some dogs are more suited to shepherding than others but it's the shepherd that brings out the best in 'em and Moses could talk to Chad as easy as talking to his brothers. I'll swear by the Blessed Virgin each one knew what t'other were thinking.

Lady Margaret made her first visit when Moses had not long been given Chad, and the lad were so smitten wi' the pup it seemed like he'd not time for his mother. She took him off to one side o' the fells and had a right old jaw wi' 'im but all he seemed bothered about were chasing after 'is new puppy. It was as if he'd left all his old life behind. She was really hurt, I could tell. She was a strong 'un though, that lady, no mistake, for she composed herself, drew in a breath, raised herself to look half a rood[19] taller than what she were and came across to me with a sunny smile. Her eyes weren't smiling though, I could tell.

"He seems to be adapting to his surroundings. You have done well, Master Lawkland," she said without a hint of bitterness but, nonetheless, an ache in her voice.

"My Lady," says I, "he might seem different to the little lad that you bid farewell to in Londesborough but that doesn't mean to say he cares any less for you now than he did then. He's been through a lot and we all have our ways of coping wi' things. But I'll tell you this, he's happy here. He'll not be mistreated, he fair enjoys his work and that little dog is his favourite companion. I think he's a symbol, like, of 'is new life, and better things to come. You cannot blame him for wanting to close the shutters down on what's happened before. Losing his father is a big loss to 'im. And he must feel like he's been chased over 'alf of the country. The responsibility of raising that dog takes his mind off things."

"And his mother is part of that old life, so he wants to forget her too," she said with a thin smile.

"Nay, don't take on so," I soothed. "I've been in your position many a

---

19. Old term for measurement.

time, coming home from my duties for Lord John. I was away from home for months sometimes. I thought me bairns would have been that happy to see me but all I got were a sniff and a nod of the head. Dogs made more fuss than them two. He'll come round in a day or two, you'll see."

She looked at me for a while and said, "It's a great comfort to me to see that he's being cared for so well. I must not be selfish, even though my heart weeps every minute of the day that I'm apart from him. It is so hard for me as Henry – Moses as you call him – is the image of his father. But it is for that reason that his lineage must be hidden. No trace of his noble birth must show and you must impress that upon him too, Master Lawkland, for I fear he has the impetuous nature of his father and that will out one day, especially if he is angered."

"All will be taken care of, My Lady; in a few months' time no one will be able to tell him apart from the rest of the barefooted shepherd boys. He's even speaking like us now," I said, ruefully.

"Alas, my ears have detected that and I must stop myself from correcting him. But what am I to do? If he speaks in the manner of a noble then he will be betrayed. No, you have done right, Master Lawkland, Tom I should say, for you are as kind to me as my own kin. May St John[20] bless you for all the troubles I have put you through."

I bowed at that. I did not want to meet her gaze as I could see tears welling in her eyes and she were that proud she would not want to show any signs of weakness. That was her way and I pitied her for that, mighty Lady though she was. My Bess would 'ave wept buckets and none would 'ave blamed her.

"Moses!" I shouted. "Get thisen ovver 'ere now and show your mother how you can work the dogs. I'll look after thee pup. Give us 'old of 'im 'ere."

Well, he were that proud showing his mother his newfound skills. That broke the ice and I saw her smile properly for the first time in months as she took stock of what he could do. She drew great pride at this shepherd-boy son that was so adaptable to any situation and as steadfast as a veteran soldier. His father would have been right proud to see him too. Maybe Moses was right, and he was looking down on him now.

Chad whimpered and yelped in my arms, eager to break free and join the

---

20. St John is the patron saint of shepherds.

older dogs as Moses shouted and whistled his commands.

Each shepherd has his own way of talking to dogs. There are four basic commands. "Come by," for a move to the left. "Away with me," for a move to the right. "Walk on," for moving for'ards, and "Lie down," for it to stop. These are all you really need to teach 'em and then when they're used to it you add in a different whistle to each command so's they soon get used to that too. Afore long you can get by with just whistling to them, to send 'em scampering up fells. The notes of the whistle are traditional and have evolved over many generations. They imitate the calls of the curlew and lapwing, birds of the high fells. To tell my dogs to go left, I give the lapwing call, and to go right, the curlew. The order to go for'ards is two short blasts and to stop is two long 'uns. Dogs can hear you clearly for half a mile or so. We've been doing that for generations and always got by on it.

Well, our Moses, he has his own system of whistling, like. I thought he'd added a few new directions like NNE or SSW to points of a compass at first but it were different than that. He had his own language. He were a wick[21] little bugger, though, and whenever you asked him how he did it, he just looked up at you and smiled to himsen. Me fatha were like that an' all. Took his secrets to the grave.

The sight of that lad working dogs was a boon for his mother, I could tell. He got a bit too big-'eaded at one bit, trying to show off working 'em too quick, and didn't see a tup break out on the edge wi' its head lowered, ready to take on the dogs. Jess, one of the oldest dogs, saw what was 'appening, circled it and nipped it on the arse. It soon got back in middle o' the flock. I scolded him for being a reckless addle-head but his mam laughed and said that he were 'is father's son all right.

She left 'appy enough, in circumstances. It were a queer do I knows, but, as we all reckon, tha's got to make the most out of any bad situation.

---

21. Intelligent, quick-witted.

Chapter 19

The Dales Folk

The rain is on the mountainside,
The beast is in the silent meadow,
The north countryside is patiently waiting again.
Blackbird is dumb in the juniper,
Lapwing shivers in the dripping thicket,
Down in the stone-faced town, one door opens.

For though the weather blow wild
I see the shepherd step up to his moorside;
And in despite of the cold
The poor farmer going to his meadow below,
Going to his meadow below.

Jake Thackray
© Leola Music Limited

THE REMOTER REGIONS OF THE DALES AND fells of the northern counties practised a method of transhumance, moving their animals on to the summer meadows and pastures high up on the hills at the first sign of spring. Vast flocks would move underway at a moment's notice, led by the goats, then the sheep, followed by the few shaggy mountain cattle. The signal for moving was not decided on by the shepherds but by the goats who instinctively knew when the pastures were ready. After all, they had occupied this windswept island before man arrived and knew better than he when the time was right. Their human followers were almost equally conditioned to this springtime ritual, as their ancestors had followed this routine for countless generations. Both the native British and the Norse newcomers had a long tradition of herding.

The lead goat had a bell attached to its collar and the sound of its clanking up the hill would be the signal for the rest of the animals to follow, observed by all the humans in the settlement who would turn out to witness this seasonal marvel.

There was something about the smell of sweet mountain thyme and the flower meadows that carried in the wind, so that the scent descended into the valley below.

First the scent of spring, then a vast caravan of animals, followed by the shepherds with their gleaming copper milking pans and their dogs in tow, was a scene so magical that it seemed to have been ordained by God. But the way that the individual flocks peeled off to occupy their own fell, where they were hefted, that was the ingenuity of man. With a little help from the sheepdogs.

As we've seen, the fells were occupied by two main tribes, the ancient British and the Norse settlers who were to a large degree easily distinguishable. The dark, stocky Britons and the fair-haired, tall, rangy Norse were different in appearance but rubbed shoulders quite easily. They had a common bond in the welfare of their animals and shared the same language based on the dialect of the later Norse settlers with a few smatterings of British words in their vocabulary.

Moses was the type of lad who'd never met a stranger and soon got to know all the families who occupied Sir Lancelot Threlkeld's land. There was one family in particular, though, the Kirkbrides, who did not fit into the characteristics of the local people. They were tall and slender with dark, almost black, glossy hair that fell down to their shoulders in tight curls. Mostly, they had pale green emerald eyes that were bewitching and had that quality that lured you into their confidence like you were their oldest friend. Yet somehow, living on the far reaches of the Threlkeld land, they did not mix easily with the others in the tiny settlements and remained a self-sufficient band. This did not deter Moses though, who soon gained acceptance into their inner circle, as his lonely fell bordered on to their mountain peaks.

There were several boys his own age but his special companion was

Geordie, a wild, exuberant youth who was full of tales about marauding Scots and his uncle's hoard of Roman and Saxon gold. They would engage in mock sword fights together and scare each other half to death with yarns about this tinker or that on the winding drovers' path, really being a Scottish spy. In the Kirkbride family, there was – no doubt about it – a great deal of hatred, if not paranoia, of their Scottish neighbours.

Folk in the Northern Marches had long memories about cattle raids from over the border and the barbaric nature of Scottish and Pictish marauders.

Bess was curious about her adoptive son's new-found friends and pressured Tom, in his position of Reeve, into gaining an invitation to the harvest feast at the Kirkbrides' homestead once summer was over.

The journey was a long one and one that Bess would not normally countenance, but curiosity got the better of her. Ralph and Luke were equally excited about attending the feast but Tom grumbled and wondered why they could not have their own at Threlkeld Hall as was the custom. He consoled himself with taking in the breathtaking scenery and let his mind drift away. He saw a tod[22] trotting to its lair and made a mental note to himself to come back with the terriers and dig it out. "Can't have that bugger taking lambkins' blood next spring," he said out loud, attracting a scolding look from Bess.

"Can't you forget about your work for one minute?" she asked.

Tom shrugged by way of an apology.

The fells hemmed them in from all sides and Tom thought it was a marvel that anyone could make a living there but the farmers clung to the mountainsides with their terraced strips of land, where they sowed oats, peas, beans and barley. The terraces were lying fallow now and the men ploughed in rich manure to condition the soil for planting next spring. A strange singing or chanting, in an old tongue that no one really understood, kept the oxen in their traces on the steeply banked hillside. Tom stopped to listen at this strange mellifluous sound and construed that there was a strange lilting inflection in this jumble of forgotten words that signified the end of each verse. He shook his head in wonder. Whatever it was, it kept the oxen content where other beasts would have baulked and teetered over the steep slopes in the traces of the heavy plough.

Moses, eager as ever, forged ahead with Luke and Ralph and beckoned

---

22. An old name for a fox.

for his parents to quicken their pace. He couldn't wait for his brothers to meet with Geordie. It was as if he needed their approval. Luke would be fine, he was sure, but he was more concerned about his taciturn elder brother who kept his counsel and took longer to make friends.

Folk were naturally wary of strangers and there was a saying in the Dales that you should winter and summer someone first before you decided upon whether you could trust them. This could not have been more apt for Ralph but he was naturally protective and, being that bit older, felt he had a responsibility for his siblings, especially Moses who, after all, had changed his identity and travelled across half the countryside to evade capture.

Ralph needn't have worried, though, as the Kirkbrides turned out in force to welcome their guests. Some of them had never left this part of the fells and were naturally curious to see Lancelot Threlkeld's reeve and his fine lady of a wife.

They lined up to greet them with grinning faces and bright twinkling eyes, looking like peas in a pod. Tom had never seen such remarkable family similarities before; they were a fine looking creed and he mused to himself that they were a lost race of people or maybe descended from the fairy folk. All apart from one, a young girl with flaming copper coloured hair, pale blue eyes and a face full of freckles.

"Who is this?" asked Bess after exchanging greetings with their host.

"That un? That's our Lénaïg," replied Simon, Geordie's uncle and leader of their small community.

"Lénaïg, that's an unusual name," said Bess, "is it a family name?"

"Naw, it's what she calls hersen," said Simon. "She were a foundling, like. We found her by Askrigg Gill when she were a little lass and couldn't understand a word she were saying, but we made out her name were Lénaïg so that's what we call her. Another mouth to feed, if we hadn't enough, but we couldn't just leave the bairn there to be eaten by wolves."

"She's very pretty. She would make a lovely handmaid for someone," cooed Bess as she smiled down on the child and threaded strands of her copper hair between her fingers.

That night, dinner was served out of doors, it being unseasonably warm and balmy for October. Several fires were lit, crackling and spitting flames into the dark, crisp air, and blankets were laid on the ground, laden with simple wholesome foods – trenchers of freshly baked bread, roast mutton, apples, juicy lustrous blackberries and late raspberries.

Everyone huddled down, covered in thick cloaks or blankets, enjoying this tasty feast and the fresh mountain air. It made a pleasant change from being indoors in a smoky chamber with thick smoke smarting your eyes. Some of the Kirkbride shepherds started up winsome tunes on beautiful flutes made from the dark wood of plum trees, to add to the cosy festive atmosphere.

Presently, Simon brought out some wine to supplement the homemade ale they had been drinking. They were served in carafes of exquisite beauty, delicate glassware, intricately patterned with gilt lids and handles. Tom gave Simon an old-fashioned look. Where had Simon managed to get such goods and such high-quality wine in this remote godforsaken place? Maybe the stories of buried Roman and Saxon gold were true. Tom decided to say nothing but Simon had detected his curiosity and needed something to distract him. He clapped his hands and presently Lénaïg sat in the middle of the group with a beautiful harp, richly inlaid with gold and mother-of-pearl. She strummed a few arpeggios and soon everyone fell silent.

Lénaïg stroked wonderful tunes out of the instrument and sang in a tongue that no one understood but whose meaning was obvious. It was as if a beautiful angel had fallen to earth and was singing a Gloria, then a Te Deum and, in the firelight, Lénaïg looked like an angel, the firelight picking out her pale luminescent complexion and golden tresses.

The normally restless boys were silent and held spellbound with these songs of another faraway land. It may have been from another world for all they knew. Indeed, Moses looked from her and then up to the starlit night, and then back to her again.

Bess broke the silence with, "Master Kirkbride, you are lucky indeed to have such a minstrel at your court. You put our simple ways at Threlkeld Hall to shame."

"She's yourn for the price of one of your 'usband's suckler calfs," said Simon, rising from his crouched position, spitting on the palm of his hand and jutting it forward for Bess to shake and seal the bargain.

Tom saved the situation by spitting on his own hand and clasping Simon's in a firm steady grip, putting his body between him and Bess so that no one could see the wrinkle of distaste on her face.

"Looks like we've got a new member of the household, my love," said Tom with a broad grin and a wink.

From that moment on, Lénaïg would not leave Bess' side and insisted on sharing the same sleeping quarters for the duration of their stay. Tom laughed at this and reckoned that she was fearful that someone might change their mind and relinquish the agreement between the two families.

Simon was happy for he thought he'd got the best of the bargain and eagerly awaited the arrival of his new calf. Lénaïg was happy as she had attached herself to the lady of Threlkeld Hall and would have fine dresses to wear. Bess was happy as she had, until now, lacked female company. Moses was happy because Luke and Ralph had bonded with Geordie quite easily. And finally, Tom was happy just to see everyone else content.

Grain was stored away safely, hay was in the mistal and they were all set to take on the ravages of a long, dark, solitary winter.

CHAPTER 20

TOM LAWKLAND -
THE WRATH OF LORD STANLEY

SEVERAL SEASONS PASSED ON FROM THE HARVEST feast at the Kirkbrides', and our Moses changed from a young stripling into a sturdy youth. My other sons were tall and raw-boned with a wiry strength but Moses was a different build altogether. He had big shoulders for a lad his age and tha' could see he were going to be barrel-chested and bull-necked when he reached full manhood.

Now, during the long darkness of winter, there's not a right lot to do. The British farmers told tales round the fire and drank themselves till they were addled in the head on winter ale and hedgerow wines. Too much activity burns up energy and to replace that you have to replenish it with food – a scarce reserve in winter. Why not slow things down and save your vigour for when it's needed, were their way o' thinking. They got through winter in a stupor, half-hibernating like a bear would.

The Norse settlers on the other hand, they had different customs and weren't at all worried about spending their energy. On a cold winter's night they'd light a roaring fire outside in the open and pit themsens against each other in trials o' strength. Our Mo were right taken wi' this and afore long he were joining in. Wrestling, hefting up great boulders above his pate and pulling ox-carts with his teeth sunk into a leather harness. Now, he were never going to be strongest at everything, as some of these fellows were very near giants, but he'd a lot of determination in him. If he couldn't do something he'd go away for hours to practise. Afore long he were able to hold his own with these lads.

And it wasn't just strength; he wanted to know about everything. He was a regular visitor to Yanwath Hall to meet that French fellow as what come up to Westmorland with us. He learned how to parley French from him and all the wiles of war and campaigning. He begged me for a sword but I'd not let 'im 'ave one. What does a shepherd boy want with a sword? Best not to arouse suspicion.

The winter of that year, when our Moses turned sixteen, were the worst I've seen in my lifetime. December came in with a cold hard frost and clear cloudless skies. I remember looking up and seeing a pale crescent moon no bigger than a fingernail clipping, and just having this feeling that something bad were going to happen. The ground were rock hard and when the snows came in January they stuck, rather than melting away like they usually do, and we got a covering of a few foot or more. The next day it snowed and the next day it snowed some more. The north-easterly wind whipped up and caused the snow to drift. In some areas it drifted into piles over ten feet high.

I was worried now. The sheep were a hardy lot and no strangers to snow, but this was different. Normally, they'd scrape away at the ice to get through to the heather, thyme, bog-myrtle and tufts of grass, but the ground were as hard as iron. I kept thinking how well they'd tupped in the autumn and what a fine flock of lambs we'd be having but this was in doubt now. The yaws wouldn't all survive in this. There was that much snow that the fells looked entirely different and the familiar landmarks were no longer there. Thank God for the dogs. They had a better instinct than me and knew where they'd have settled.

There was nothing else for it, we had to get to the sheep and risk our own lives in doing so. No sheep meant no food and wages. We harnessed up the few Dales' ponies we had and got the sledges out of the mistal and loaded them up with gurt big sacks of hay.

The going was heavy and the snow covered the ponies' fetlocks. Soon, icicles formed on the flanks of the sweating ponies but I've always admired their strength and stamina. They'd go on as long as we bid them.

The dogs had a hard time of it too, sinking deep into the snow but bounding out again, leaping like salmon determined to get to their spawning ground. I couldn't tell where the mountain paths were but the dogs knew and guided us all upwards, man and pony alike, struggling and heaving up the fell. It were best to keep moving; as soon as you stopped the chill wind hit your sweaty flanks and the cold bit right through to your bones, your very soul, at least that's what it felt like. These familiar mountains that provided our living were a desolate, cruel place in the depths of this icy grip.

Just after halfway up the fell, the dogs started yelping and scratching away at a big snow drift. I'd no idea how deep it was but it was big 'un all right. There was a snow hole where the sheep had been breathing through, so down there somewhere were our yaws. The dogs scratched away furiously and me and my lads, we took the mattocks and spades off of the sledge and started digging away furiously too. We were hasty though; it was hard work and we needed to plan it better and we'd forgotten about the ponies. It was a crime not to feed them first after all the hard work they'd given us. Ralph and Luke fed the hungry beasts while me and our Moses formulated a plan.

The wind had been so chilling that the first few feet of snow was more or less compacted into ice. We took the mattocks and carved channels into the snow so that we formed ice blocks. Then, using the ponies that had now been rested and fed, we harnessed them to the blocks and pulled them away across the fellside before releasing these icy wedges, sending them tumbling down the fell. Once this layer were removed, the snow was much softer and we made quick progress.

I'll never forget the pitiful look on the face of the yaws when we pulled them out. I felt how I'd let them down somehow. What had happened was they'd taken shelter from the wind behind a dry-stone wall and huddled together to keep warm. The snow had drifted over them and this in itself had provided shelter for them, out of the bitter wind inside their snow hole. But there was no food of course and we needed to get nourishment into these expectant mothers – and quick. Most took no time in snatching at the sweet-smelling hay and sating their hunger but some of the shearlings, the ones that had been born the previous spring, had never seen hay before and didn't know what to make of it. There was not a lot we could do about this. We had to leave them to it and find the next flock of sheep. Our Moses stood there counting – yan, tan, tether, mether, pip and so on. I reckon we saved fifty that day.

We repeated this pattern every day while the snows lasted throughout January to mid-February, returning home to a plate of warm mutton stew, slumped down in front of a peat fire, absolutely exhausted. Character-building stuff, I told the lads, but they said they'd rather not go through it again.

Every day we found more and more dead sheep, frozen solid by the wintry embrace of the snow queen and every day the wolves grew bolder. They never had such a harvest. My lads loved the sheep that much. It was as if one of their family had died. Well, what can I say? We made the best of a bad job but even lambing time didn't bring its usual feeling of wellbeing as we knew our stock would be down that year.

In February, Sir Lancelot came to visit us. He'd been cut off by the snow drifts until then. He was very grim faced. Other fells had been worse hit than us by the sound of it and he said we'd have to buy in some stock that summer from Masham sheep fair. He wanted me to assess what we'd need after lambing time was over, and tally up with him.

When it came to going to Masham, the biggest sheep fair in the land, I were really excited. Sheep were herded down from Scotland to be sold for grazing on our rough pastures and our northern sheep were eagerly bought by farmers from as far away as Suffolk and Sussex and places I could only imagine. I knew what I had in mind to buy and I also wanted a big Norfolk tup to improve our stock, but Sir Lancelot, he reckoned I shouldn't go. He knew I'd be recognized by many there and didn't want anyone knowing I was working for him for fear they'd put two and two together and lead them to our Moses.

Instead, our Moses was to go with the Kirkbrides, who knew how to drive a hard bargain. He reckoned that no one would recognize our Moses from the seven year old lordling Henry Clifford, that had fled Skipton all those years ago. On the day they left to go for the fair, I had another one of my funny premonitions and begged Sir Lancelot not to send him, but he laughed at me for being an old woman. He said the experience would do him good.

Well, word got out right enough. Our Moses, being Moses, got stuck in at the village campball[23] and impressed everyone with his strength and then someone persuaded him to enter the wrestling competition. Talk about attracting attention to yoursen.

Most of the sheep fairs have wrestling contests and the winner gets a prize ram so tha' can imagine there's quite a few takers. He'd bested the regulars and arse-ended the old champion in the final bout, positively embarrassing the fellow. So it was inevitable, summat were said about this shepherd

---

23. A rough medieval game, the forerunner of football.

lad that looked a spit-drawn image of a Clifford, so's that clarty old villain, Lord Stanley, heard about it and put two and two together.

Rumours have a way of spreading far and wide across North Country and two o' the most popular tales were what had become of the Clifford lads and the duping of Lord Stanley by old Gasper. He'd not lived that last one down and he were the laughing stock o' the North, common folk and nobles alike.

Try as he might he couldn't lay his hands on old Gasper or his money, after he'd bought his own sheep back offen him. Schemer as he was, he weren't going to get more land from the King wi' that sort o' reputation. That's when I reckon he hatched on his plan to capture this shepherd lad to restore his damaged pride. That sort wouldn't 'ave bothered whether he'd got right lad or not, he'd have made some tale or other to suit his plot and then get the King to reward him for his troubles.

He sent two of his men to search for us. Dickon Hoccleve and Edward Lambert were their names and they were a right mismatched pair. Dickon were a local lad and had a bit more about him but Edward were from service of Stanley's Cheshire estates and uncomfortable in these unfamiliar surroundings. He were a brave man and a skilled archer but he saw something behind every stone and bush and were not best suited to our coarse boulder-strewn fells. I were told later that they'd had rough treatment wherever they'd enquired of us and folk would not afford them 'ospitality or shelter.

We were penning sheep up for shearing, one fell at a time, me, Ralph, Luke and our Moses, when they hove into view. Two soldiers, a long way from home, never bring glad tidings so's I warned the lads to be on their guard and stay tight-lipped.

Dickon, the taller of the two, comes up first like, and asks us how we do. Me and the lads, we just nods like, and carries on. This Dickon, he comes closer and says how he's looking for a Yorkshire lad what 'as gone missing. I stopped. I stared down on him and said there were no missing lads here. These were my sons and we'd work to do for Sir Lancelot Threlkeld. I told him to report to Sir Lancelot at the Hall if he 'ad any such questions – this were his land after all.

He then says, "Tha's from Yorkshire, aren't tha'?" and I says, "Tha' thinks I'm the missing lad?" He says, "What about that one there?" pointing to our Moses – "he could be the missing young gentleman my Lord is seeking."

"What, that big barefoot lummox?" I says. "That's our Mo, he's no more of a gentleman than I am."

Then t'other one, nervy little bugger, stepped for'ards and drew his sword in front of our Moses. I did nowt but took a deep breath for I reckoned they weren't about to harm him, but our Mo, he grabbed this Edward Lambert by the wrist of his sword-arm and squeezed. It were a gentle squeeze at first, just enough to contain 'im but then our Mo looked into the soldier's flickering eyes, grinning, increasing the pressure. He kept the pressure on and raised the sword afore twisting it downward with a final steely squeeze that had the blade dropping from his hand, quivering point downwards into the turf.

I picked the sword up and handed it to Dickon – t'other fellow's arm were limp and if it weren't I wouldn't 'ave trusted 'im with it any roads.

"Tha' knows what they say," I laughed. "Yorkshire born. Yorkshire bred. Strong in arm. And thick in 'ead!

"Now, I reckon it's time you and yon brave warrior went to pay your respects to my Lord Lancelot at Yanwath Hall. It's in that direction, over yon. We'll not keep you any longer."

Well, they made to leave and disappeared over brow o' the next fell but I knew they'd be back.

At dusk, they returned. They approached, warily at first, but came to the foot o' the fell, sure enough, and hailed me.

"Hand the lad over to us and we'll spare the rest of you. It's him that we want," shouted Dickon.

I laughed and said they could come and get 'im.

Dickon moved closer and said, "It's him, right enough. I weren't sure at first but when he got hold o' Edward's hand here and I saw that look in his eye I knew it were Butcher Clifford's son. Last time I saw a face like that I were at Ferrybridge where he drowned half o' our vanguard. That's Blackface Clifford's boy all right and I don't plan on leaving here without him."

I were that mad I shouted back into the failing light, "He's my son and you're not taking him anywhere. I'm the only Fatha he's got on this God's earth and I'd like to see the man that'll take him away from me."

Dickon looked at his mate and said, "Have it your own way. Edward here's a fine archer and he'll pick off every one of you come dawn. There's no way down that fell and we're staying put."

At that, they set up camp for the night and lit a fire. It were a damp June evening and midges were out in force. They didn't bother us, as us shepherds rub lanolin on to our face and arms so's they just get stuck there till we scrape 'em off. It were different for the soldiers though and midges were eating lumps out of 'em. They were in for an uncomfortable night.

I whispered to the boys to be of good cheer and told 'em we'd be all right and not to try 'owt foolish. When it were proper dark, I motioned for them to follow me a bit higher up, where the beck came splashing down the fell. As quiet as we could, we dammed the river bed and diverted the water to where the soldier lads were camped. It were only a tiny beck but there'd be enough water to soften the ground and slow their progress towards us by morning.

I tried to get the lads to sleep but they only managed a few fitful snatches. A fine drizzle did not help matters much in that direction but the good Lord sent it us as a boon, for a damp bowstring is no good to even the surest of archers.

At dawn, they hailed us again but they were not so confident now.

God forgive me, but I cursed them roundly and beckoned them on. I got me, Ralph and Luke wi' our mastiff out in front and stood firm wi' our stout ash poles in our 'ands. I made Moses stay directly behind us for fear of arrows and he were proper mad, straining to get into the fray but I wouldn't hear of it. Bowman would be of no use any road, until he got to closer quarters. I don't mind saying, my 'eart were pounding and blood were fair thumping in me temples. Nowt for it but a deep breath and try to stay calm. A burst o' temper might o' been death o' all of us.

As they advanced, Moses whistled to the sheepdogs so they circled behind the two bedraggled henchmen. They advanced more slowly then, looking over their shoulders to check what was happening wi' grinning, crouching, wolfish dogs. They were not so confident now and when they got to within fifty yards of us, they were checked by the marsh we'd made by damming the beck. There was no way round; they were soon up to their knees in cloying, bubbling mud that sucked at their very souls. That were my signal to act and I shouted at the mastiff to attack. It covered squelchy ground in seconds and soon 'ad 'old of Dickon, pressing 'im into the mud. T'other fellow looked round to see if he could get away but he were too fast in the ground. He stood there, just time enough to piss his britches afore a gurt jagged boulder hurtled through the air and stoved his skull in. He were fair riggweltered.

I looked back and saw it were our Moses as had thrown the stone and he had the killing face on, no doubt about it. He were down that fell, wading through mud afore anyone could stop him and joined in wi' the mastiff, who was mauling that fellow Dickon while Moses was throttling at the same time. The cries for mercy were pitiful but the man had to die. Moses pulled a knife from the soldier's belt, knelt over him and stabbed him over and over again, great spurts o' blood arcing in the air.

I grabbed his bloody upturned arm, just as it were about to plunge into Dickon's chest again, and took the blade off of him.

"There, there, lad. It's over now," I said to his blood smattered face. "He'll not try and harm us again." His face were purple and twisted in anger though. I've never seen such a rage. Some might say it's the Clifford blood in 'im but it seemed to me he wanted revenge. Revenge against a mad world that had thrown his life into turmoil and would not leave him alone, even when he'd found peace. Poor bugger.

And then I turned round and our Luke were ligged out on the ground, moaning his 'ead off. Yon archer must have loosed off one of his arrows for it had gone through his chaperon, and were still embedded in it close to his right ear. There were blood trickling down his neck. All sorts went thumping through my head. I'm ashamed to say, I said to meself, "I've saved one adopted son only for a true one to be mortally slain." May God in His heaven forgive me for the thought.

I knelt by his side. He looked sideways and said, "Fatha, it's going dark. Fatha, where are you? Is that someone I can hear singing? Is that an angel?" and then convulsed into a heaving that racked his whole body. I wept like a woman.

And then he laughed. His face contorted into a stupid grin and he laughed and laughed and sat upright, clutching his sides. I kicked him and called him a daft beggar but he just laughed some more, taking off his chaperon and wiping a trickle of blood from the nick in his ear. That was our Luke for you.

Luke's jesting aside, it were a bad business right enough, but Sir Lancelot knew how to handle it. He paid a purse of gold for our Scottish neighbour, Lord Douglas, to take blame for it. I can remember Douglas coming to the Hall and the hackles standing up on everyone's neck just at the sight o' this ginger-haired bandit. Lancelot were calm enough about it all though and had a bit of a laugh wi' the Scotch fellow. Between 'em, they hatched up this plot that Dickon and Edward had strayed onto Scottish lands searching for us and had met their death by his men's hand. Seeing their livery, he had realized the mistake and would ask Lord Stanley for a ransom for the return of their corpses. He'd not get one, they knew, but Lord Stanley would have apoplexy at the barefaced cheek of it all.

CHAPTER 21

THE NUT-BROWN MAID

Whatever befall, I never shall
Of this thing be upbraid:
But if ye go, and leave me so,
Then have ye me betrayed.
Remember you wele, how that ye dele;
For if ye, as ye said,
Be so unkind to leave behind
Your love, the Nut-brown Maid,
Trust me truly that I shall die
Soon after ye be gone:
For, in my mind, of all mankind
I love but you alone.

Traditional Poem – Anon.

MOSES WOULD OFTEN SIT ASTRIDE THE SUMMIT of Blencathra, as the native British called it, or Saddleback Fell as it was more commonly known. From there he had a panoramic view across the Threlkeld estates and on a clear day, he could see Great Whernside in Yorkshire, part of the route he had originally taken with Tom to get here. He often mused about what was happening across in the lands of his father's Yorkshire estates, but had no real desire to take up his old life, despite the privileges it would afford him.

On this particular day he was watching the scene below with some amusement. A hunting party was stirring below. Horns were blowing and the pack of hounds were yelping and barking, making enough noise to warn off any game within the next twenty leagues. Sir Lancelot was hosting the hunt party and he had some important guests. Moses' mother, Lady Margaret, was there too, but he had been warned to stay out of the way. She was spending more time with Sir Lancelot than with him now when she came to visit the county, but he cared little about it. He was a man doing a man's job and answered to none but Tom.

The horses were skittish and keen to be off. It was strange to see normally docile, well-trained animals change character once they were assembled in the field. It was the herding instinct that made them behave wildly like this and there was a frisson of excitement in the air that affected horses, dogs and men alike.

Ralph and Luke had been enlisted to scout ahead for the hunt's quarry and it was Ralph who came tearing down the fell first to say that he had stalked a large stag with eight point antlers, close to Skiddaw Forest. Ralph was no horseman and Moses laughed at his attempts to spur on his horse downhill whilst trying to stay seated. "Lay back in the saddle brother," he said to no one but himself, but the words were snatched by the wind and blown far across to Hallsfell.

Lancelot received the news of the stag with great enthusiasm and blew three short blasts on his horn to gain everyone's attention. With halloos and whooping the throng of gentry broke their steeds into a canter and followed the baying dogs across the brown and purple fells, resplendent in their autumn colours.

Moses watched the stag raise its noble head in the direction of the hunt and followed its progress as it trotted into the cover of Skiddaw Forest, its does following obediently behind. By the time the hunting party arrived, it emerged nimbly through the far side of the forest and then picked its way up and over the far side of the fell.

There was something comical about the scene enacted below. The dogs were slow in picking up the scent as it was a wet drizzly day and the fewterer expended great amounts of energy and oaths preventing stray hounds wandering off along the wrong trail. The hunters didn't mind, though, and seemed to be in a great state of excitement. From what Moses could see, it was more about who had the finest apparel and best mount. If they had been really serious about getting venison for dinner, then Ralph could have provided that with just one arrow when he stalked the red deer earlier on in the morning.

He could pick his mother out, her fine popinjay green cloak billowing behind as she urged her palfrey on. She had a good seat, and could hold her own with the more adventurous men, who treated these events as a training exercise for warfare.

It wasn't long before they reached the forest and the whipper-in fanned the dogs out in a crescent formation before they plunged into its depths with the riders walking the horses on close behind.

After a long while and a lot of noise, the party broke free of the forest and the hounds streamed up the fellside, baying for all they were worth. They were on the scent and Moses heard the dogs cry out as they picked up the trail, barking out the directions to take and no doubt shouting out encouragement to each other. He smiled as they disappeared from view and bent down to pat his own dogs' heads, who were watching the scene with as much interest as him and adding their own chorus to the goings on. He was about to leave and return to his hut when he saw a rider emerge from the nearest side of the woods. A young woman by the look of it, dressed in russet hunting attire with a tawny brown cloak, seated on a dappled mare. She looked into the distance for a minute or two then circled her horse around and turned back into the forest. She was clearly lost.

Moses whistled for his dogs and sent them ahead as he descended the fell with all the sure-footed agility of a mountain goat. He sent them into the forest and knew that they would follow the path of the rider and lead her back to him. He waited at the edge of the forest and climbed to a seat in the forked trunk of a gnarled old oak, waiting patiently. When she came into view, framed by the russet branches of the beech trees, his heart stopped. He was looking at a Madonna, a beautiful painting, with the colours of an artist's palette picking out every autumn hue of red, orange, brown, sienna and gold in the background. She was the most stunning thing he had ever seen. Dark hair framed a beautiful oval face with doe-like pale brown eyes that were flecked with olive. Her skin had a beautiful milky texture and her lips were a perfect rosebud. She opened them into a wide smile that set her eyes sparkling when she saw Moses reclining in the tree. He looked on dumbfounded. He took in her beautiful nut-brown velvet clothes and rich worsted cloak. He took in her beauty. He took in the way his dogs looked up at her adoringly and for the first time in his life, he did not know what to say and felt rather stupid about his roosting place in the tree. Should he explain to her? Should he get down first?

She saved him the answer for she spoke first. "So, this is my gallant rescuer? Your dogs have been telling me all about you, haven't you?" she said, setting the fawning dogs off on another spree of tail-wagging.

Her voice was beautiful too. She enunciated every word very clearly and earnestly and it minded Moses of the sound of tinkling icicles clinging to the tufts of grass by a mountain stream.

"Well, aren't you going to get down?" she asked.

He started, then slid down the trunk of the tree and mumbled, "My Lady, I am at your service," as he held the reins of her horse. The sound that came out of his mouth was gruff and had a foggy quality. The exact opposite to her voice. He had tried to make it sound like his mother's but it did not, would not, come out that way.

He met her gaze, then looked down at the sodden leaves on the forest floor. He looked up and tried again. "My Lady, your clothes are wet and you must be tired, I will lead you to shelter." It came out wrong again and he felt awkward and churlish. He looked down at his calloused hands, his rough clothes and big hulking frame. She must think him an oaf. A rustic, ill-mannered, loutish knave of a peasant. It was another first for him; he wished he had spent more time conversing with his mother and learning the courtly language that she believed, one day, he would need.

"I *am* rather tired," she laughed, and just the sound of her voice set his emotions racing again. He had to take control, take the initiative, or she would think him a gawk. He had originally intended to point her back on the trail of her companions but now he could not let that happen. He didn't know why, but he needed to squeeze every minute out of this encounter.

"I'm afraid Sir Lancelot and your friends are long gone, My Lady. Your cloak is wet and will no longer afford you any protection. I will take you to my mother at Threlkeld Hall. She will dry your clothes and feed you. My brothers will tend to your horse. My name is Moses by the way. My father is Sir Lancelot's man."

"Moses, what a virtuous name," she said. "I've never met anyone by that name before."

He longed to say that his real name was Henry and that he was really Sir John Clifford's son, on an equal footing to her. Even if he dared, he reasoned, she wouldn't believe him. She would just laugh at this illiterate peasant who spoke in a strange rustic tongue.

"Well, Moses, I am very pleased to make your acquaintance and right glad that you have been my saviour today. My name is Anne and I am eternally grateful for the service you do me. I feel safe in the protection of such a strong young gentleman and cannot wait to meet the mother that bore you."

He blushed at this but as he led her homeward, her natural grace put him at his ease and she made him feel important by asking him questions about the scenery and local customs, his family and his duties on Sir Lancelot's estate.

By the time he got to Threlkeld Hall he was sorry that this intimate part of their relationship would end. He would now have to share her conversation with others.

His mother came fussing out to greet them. "Who is this fine nut-brown maid you bring home, son?" she asked of Moses whilst curtsying to Anne, taking in her fine clothes.

"This is Anne, Mother," Moses replied in the clearest voice he could articulate. Behind her, Ralph sniggered at his attempt to speak like the gentry.

Bess scolded him out of the way and beckoned Anne and Moses inside. She took Anne's cloak and shouted for Lénaïg to come and attend their guest, ordering her to bring fresh clothes from the linen chest and warm them by the fire. Lénaïg took one look at Moses standing moonstruck in front of Lady Anne and took on a skittish mood, her plaited hair flicking like an angry tail in his direction as she turned on her heel to fetch the warm clothes.

She returned, stamping her feet like an angry mare, and said to Moses, "What makes you stay inside a proper house so long, aren't you fretting after your sheep?"

Bess took the clothes from her and arranged them in front of the fire, beckoning Moses to stoke it, and then turned again to Lénaïg.

"Go and prepare the master chamber for My Lady, she will want to change into these soon, and then put the broth on to heat. I am fearful My Lady will take on a fever."

Lénaïg flashed an angry look at Moses as she left the room and Anne, sensing the current in the air said, "I am sorry to cause your household so much trouble, it was foolish of me to lose my way."

Bess replied with, "My Lady, we are honoured with your presence. It is not often we have such visitors to our home. I was once in service to Lady Margaret at Brough Castle and sorely miss the times I had with her. Your company is a pleasant diversion from an otherwise dull existence with these hulking sons of mine. Moses, whatever was I thinking of, Sir Lancelot will be worried that he has lost one of his charges. Take your father's horse and ride out to him."

Moses was startled out of his reverie. "Let Ralph go, for he is the finer horseman."

Ralph did not stir for nearly a full minute, but seeing the look of grim determination on his brother's face, reached for his cloak and headed for the door, giving Moses a knowing look over his shoulder. They could hear Ralph's coarse laugh at the other side of the door and, to cover their embarrassment, Bess said, "What fine clothes, what beautiful velvet, oh and look at the black pearls on the sleeve. I said to myself when I saw you, oh what a lovely colour; it really suits your complexion. The nut-brown maid."

"Yes, Mother, and I did find her in the forest," said Moses, feeling a lot more at ease now that Ralph was out of the way. "A fitting find for the season. Mother Nature has gifted her to us as a portent. Maybe winter will not be so harsh this year."

Lénaïg returned, looking at the group with open hostility, so Bess decided to wait on Lady Anne herself and change her into the warm aired clothes. Besides, she would not trust Lénaïg with this fine velvet. The mood she was in she was likely to scorch it on the fire. She scolded herself for not noticing the attachment the girl clearly had for Moses sooner. The girl was burnt with love but dare not tell. That was a relationship she would have to nip in the bud, not that Moses seemed to reciprocate. He was riveted to the dining hall floor like a moonstruck calf, waiting for his nut-brown maid to return. Normally, he did not tarry any more than he had to indoors, claiming the atmosphere was too stifling for him. Now, he was under their feet.

When she returned, Moses had washed his hands and face and was laying out a wooden bowl and a pewter spoon ready for the warming broth.

"Nay, Moses my son, why not let Lénaïg do that?" enquired his mother, although she already knew the answer.

"Why, us Lawkland men are not helpless when it comes to victuals and cooking, Mother. We have to tend for ourselves all summer long and there are no women around on the fells to care for our needs. I was just being hospitable as I feel responsible for Lady Anne, me being the one that found her."

Anne replied, "And right glad I am too. I have often heard speak of your famous Northern hospitality. What a tale I will have to tell when I return home. That of a dashing, handsome young man saving me from the perils of the forest and leading me to this enchanting old hall. This broth is the best I have ever tasted. I will be sad when this adventure has to end."

The prospect of the adventure ending saddened Moses too. He was comforted, though, when his mother said to Anne, "I fear that you may have picked up a chill or a fever on those bleak fells. I cannot countenance you returning to Yanwath tonight in this dank air. You must stay with us until your strength is restored. I will send word to Lady Margaret, she will understand. Moses, go and fetch some game from the larder for supper. We will make a feast of it tonight in honour of the nut-brown maid."

When he left, Anne asked his mother about his childhood and how they came to live here. Bess was guarded at first, but warmed to the task when she came to the subject of naming him.

"I wanted something different that would make him stand out. Every man child is named William or Thomas or Henry or what-you-will and I have always liked the name Moses. The priest tells me he was a strong leader of his people and I think that one day my Moses will be just that."

Anne looked at her quizzically. There was more to this shepherd than Bess was telling her. Maybe he was the natural-born son of Sir Lancelot or some other noble lord. Why install the family in the Threlkeld's ancestral home? He was a fine-looking youth, though, and this time it was her turn to blush. She caught herself staring in his direction whenever he was in the room. Ladies of her station would not consort with such types ordinarily, but she reasoned that she was well chaperoned by Bess and no harm would come of it.

That night, Moses slept on a settle in the main hall. His brother, Ralph, was there too and disturbed him with his snoring but he soon drifted off into a fitful sleep. He dreamt of an enchanted forest bathed in blue light and of

Anne losing her way, desperately trying to find her way out of the tangled thicket. She was wearing her tawny cloak and there was a strange singing in the background, in a tongue that he did not recognize. Then, she saw him and smiled. The singing continued in the strange tongue but this time it was Anne that was doing the singing and he listened rapturously to her clear crystal voice and the tinkling of icicles. The dream repeated itself several times but on the final occasion, at the part when she recognized him, he was standing in the dark forest wearing a long black cloak. And when he removed the cloak she saw he was dressed as a fine lord. He was Lord Henry Clifford of Craven, Earl of Westmorland and heir to the Vescy estates.

A rough hand shook his shoulder and brought him reluctantly out of his dream. It was Lénaïg.

"Been dreaming about your lady love, have you? You were moaning in your sleep. While you're biding here you might as well make yoursen useful and go and milk the cow for breakfast. I'll stoke the fire up. Can't have milady catching a chill now, can we?"

In the event, it was several days before Anne returned to Yanwath Hall. Not on account of her health but on account of the appalling weather. The rain had not let up for two solid days and then, when it had abated, they had to allow time for the floodwater to drain away from the mountain paths. Typical Lakeland weather.

Moses still felt a little awkward talking to Anne but her natural manner did all it could to make matters easier for him. He volunteered to take her back and his brothers could not hide their mirth at his obvious attachment. Lénaïg was nowhere to be seen.

The young couple chattered easily along the way but felt the pace slowing down as they reluctantly got closer to Yanwath. His mother, Lady Margaret, was there to greet them and gave a surprised look to see her son at this unexpected encounter. A young nobleman spurred his horse on and made to take the bridle from Moses' hand, trying to nudge him out of the way with the flank of his horse. Moses stood firm and stared insolently at the richly attired young man. His mother took the bridle from him and led the horse away, with Anne looking over her shoulder at her new companion. Moses looked on as his mother took away from him the person that was now the most precious in his life, without a word.

"Farewell my gallant knight!" shouted Anne as she was led away. Moses looked at the receding figure longingly. This was too much for the richly dressed young man who spurred his horse directly at Moses again. With a piercing whistle, Moses had his dogs snapping at the horse's flanks and the beast reared, pawing the air. The rider was immediately unseated and landed resoundingly on the squelchy turf, the wind knocked out of him. Notwithstanding this, Moses leaned down and picked him up with one hand scrunching at his doublet and the other squeezing tight on his scrotum.

"Poxy gentleman, what good are your fine clothes and noble charger now? Tell me now, or has the cat got thy tongue?" There was no response from the gasping victim. "Do not ever stand in my way again or next time I'll remove these," he said, squeezing tighter on the young man's codpiece. He threw him back in the mud with a final, "And you go and tell that to Sir Lancelot Threlkeld and My Lady bloody Clifford. They know where to find me."

A tall, cloaked figure raced to the scene and started to unsheathe his sword to protect the young man lying prone on the floor, but hesitated when he recognized the angry face of the young shepherd.

"It can't be," he said to himself. Robert, the brother of John Clifford, had long been in exile to escape the vengeful arm of Edward IV. Now that he was back in England he was shocked to see this young man, clearly his nephew, bearing the exact features of his long-dead brother.

CHAPTER 22

LÉNAÏG

Come live with me and be my love,
And we will all the pleasures prove
That valleys, groves, hills, and fields,
Woods, or steepy mountain yields.
And we will sit upon rocks,
Seeing the shepherds feed their flocks,
By shallow rivers to whose falls
Melodious birds sing madrigals.
And I will make thee beds of roses
And a thousand fragrant posies,
A cap of flowers, and a kirtle
Embroidered all with leaves of myrtle;
A gown made of the finest wool
Which from our pretty lambs we pull;
Fair lined slippers for the cold,
With buckles of the purest gold;
A belt of straw and ivy buds,
With coral clasps and amber studs;
And if these pleasures may thee move,
Come live with me, and be my love.
The shepherd swains shall dance and sing
For thy delight each May morning:
If these delights thy mind may move,
Then live with me and be my love.

Christopher Marlowe

It did not take long for Lady Margaret Clifford to seek him out. Moses was at Threlkeld helping his father and brothers build a new dry stone wall enclosure for the sheep. The rhythm of their work together was soothing but was soon shattered when he was summoned to the Hall.

"Just what did you think you were doing, you young fool?" demanded his mother by way of greeting.

He stood there, saying nothing but seething, the slow fuse of his temper smouldering.

"We thought to keep you here out of harm's sake. We told you to keep away from the hunting party and what do you do? You court a high-born young lady and assault her brother like a common ruffian."

Bess and Lénaïg cowered in the kitchen, not knowing whether to quit the scene or to quietly go about their duties. Lady Margaret had not even acknowledged their presence and in her present state probably did not know they were there.

Still Moses said nothing. He just looked intently at his mother.

"What's more, you were recognized," she continued.

This elicited no reaction from Moses.

"As you seem to have no concern over this, perhaps it would interest you to know that the man who recognized you was your uncle, Robert Clifford. He is well displeased at your behaviour. Too long have you tarried here. Your wild character needs to be held in check." Then, apropos of nothing, she added, "Furthermore, Sir Lancelot and I are to be married."

Moses flinched at this but still remained grimly silent.

Margaret continued. "Sir Lancelot and your uncle say that your existence is not so much of a threat to the King now. Would he know of your circumstances, your life would not be under threat. The Bollings have been pardoned and have their lands back now and Gloucester does much good work in the North. The land is healing. It is time for you to come back to where you rightly belong and Lancelot will be as a father to you. He will school you in courtly ways."

This was too much for Moses. His face turned crimson and he roared a full tirade at her.

109

"A father to me? Why do I need another father? My father is in heaven and I have an earthly father here, better than any man you name. A man that is kind and gentle and that has risked his life to raise me. No, he has not courtly ways but he truly loves me as a father should. I have a mother there," he said, pointing to Bess. "That lady stood trembling there for fear you take me away from her, she has been more of a mother to me than you ever were or would be.

"As for being pardoned by that traitor, Edward, would he grant me my lands and title back?" he demanded.

Margaret, shocked at this outburst, could do nothing but answer quietly, "No, I do not believe so, Henry, but your birth would be acknowledged and with the support of Richard of Gloucester you may be granted..."

Moses interrupted her. "Moses, Mother. My name is plain Moses Lawkland until such a time as I am restored to my lands and titles. I will not take charity from Gloucester. I am sick of hearing what good works this man Gloucester does! That man and his brother, the bastard[24] are murderers. I have sworn to be avenged of them. My time will come. It is written in the stars and when that time comes I will return. I will have my land and all that belongs to me returned. Go back to your Sir Lancelot and I hope you are both right happy together," he said through gritted teeth, "but when I come back to you, back to polite society, I will be *his* Lord and things will be different.

"Now, right now, I am staying here with these wild people. I am wild like them. I have killed two men already and will kill more, if people try and harm us. Let the King and all his courtly people know that."

He stormed out of the door and strode up the fell to his shepherd's hut, his dogs following behind at a distance without being summoned by his whistle.

Margaret stood there, stunned, for minutes, her lips moving but saying nothing. Then she noticed Bess and her bottom lip trembled. Bess instinctively reached out and put her arms around her to offer comfort.

"Have I been such a bad mother, Bess?" she asked, choking with tears.

---

24. It was rumoured that Edward IV was actually born of his mother's adulterous affair with an Archer and was not the legitimate son of the Duke of York)

"Nay, you have made the biggest sacrifice of all, My Lady, I know full well, but the boy has grown into a man now and is strong-willed. He speaks harsh words but he does not mean them. He is a gentle soul, really, but I think his loins have been stirred by meeting Lady Anne. He wants to be with his own kind now, but wants to do it on his terms. He is very proud and there is no point trying to gainsay him. The only one to talk him round will be Tom, but even he would counsel to let his heels cool down."

"He is so like his father," smiled Margaret, wiping the tears away with the heel of her hand.

"And you are to be married again, my lady," smiled Bess. "God blesses you with such a fine man as Sir Lancelot. Enjoy your wedding preparations and fear not for your son. He will come good. I am sure of it."

Unnoticed by the others, Lénaïg slipped quietly into the scullery. She wrapped some bread, cheese and fruit in a cloth and took a flask of elderberry wine from the cellar, Moses' favourite. She left by the scullery door without her cloak and slowly followed the path of Moses up to Blencathra.

She took her time, smiling at the stunted trees and the heather-tinted moorside as she climbed the stony trail. The dogs noticed her first and came to greet her but Moses did nothing to acknowledge her presence. This was his fell and no one else was welcome.

She sat some distance away, saying nothing, just giving him the odd sidelong glance. After a while she stared more directly at him, watching for the moment when his anger would subside, as she knew it would.

The sun was low on the horizon before he stirred, giving her a faint flicker of recognition.

This was her cue. "Hard, isn't it?" she said. "Not knowing where you belong."

He looked at her.

"Not knowing where tha' fits in. I feel the same way tha' does, in a way. Not knowing from where I came, but Master Tom and Bess have been good to me. I must admit, I thought there was something different about tha' but I didn't know tha' was Lady Margaret's son. Tha's kept

111

that one quiet. Tha's a dark horse all right."

Moses laughed mockingly, but the spell was broken and the anger had dispersed.

"I don't know how tha' feels, but sometimes I just wish I belonged to Master and Mistress properly. Not being of their blood like, sometimes it makes me feel an outsider, kind as they are to me. But tha's spoiled. They can't do enough for thee."

Moses shot her an angry look but she just laughed.

"Here, want some of this?" she said, unwrapping the food at his feet and uncorking the wine.

Moses hadn't eaten since breakfast and the hunger pangs cramped his stomach.

"Have some wine first, it's your favourite," she said, pouring it into a horned cup.

He drank greedily and broke off a piece of cheese. She tore off a piece of bread and fed it to him a morsel at a time, pressing the wine cup to his lips in between. It was the most sensual gesture that he had ever experienced. The heady wine increased the physicality of the moment and he looked at her properly for the first time. Tresses of her gleaming copper hair had come loose and he smoothed it away from her face. He noticed her eyes, really beautiful eyes betwixt blue and green, and it minded him of the colour of his mother's popinjay cloak, but he quickly brushed that thought aside. She had an elf-like, childish face with a light dusting of freckles. But it had that knowing look. She knew what he was thinking; only he wasn't thinking clearly at all. He wanted her then, but hesitated.

"I have never been so close to you," she whispered and looked into his eyes. She was kneeling in front of him and proffered some more wine. His hand reached out around her yielding waist and she let it rest there for a while before removing it, slipping away laughingly.

"Is that how you fine gentlemen behave?" she teased. There was a tense silence, then she stared at him and recited:

"When thou ran, or wrestled, or putted the stone,
And came off the victor, my heart was not forlorn:
Thy every sport, manly, gave pleasure to me,
For none can putt, or wrestle, or run as swift as thee".

Adapted from The Gentle Shepherd
Allan Ramsay

Moses blushed, his burning cheeks betraying his emotion and ravelled doubts. The verse was obviously something she had rehearsed and she was making her intentions clear. He looked at her and noticed for the first time how her hips angled provocatively on her coltish frame as she shifted her weight from foot to foot.

His ardour was aroused and his heart was pounding. She watched him before slowly sitting down next to him, plucking at the couch grass. She plaited it into a coronet.

"A crown for the earl of Westmorland," she said, placing it on his tawny head. He put his hands on her shoulders and pressed them gently into the grass before kissing her. A long yearning kiss that came from his soul as much as from his loins. They made love all that night under the starlit sky, passionately, tenderly, and often. Nothing else in the world mattered apart from their time together.

In the early morning, they came down from the fell together hand in hand, he still wearing his grass-plaid coronet and she with a radiant smile. She gave him a lingering kiss before returning to the Hall through the scullery door with a sultry look. He stood there looking at the door after she had gone, all the anger from the previous day forgotten.

It was a full six months before it was obvious that Lénaïg was with child and Bess took her to one side.

"Who is the father?" she asked, but Lénaïg was silent on the matter.

"Was it one of the village boys?"

Still nothing from Lénaïg.

"Oh, by the Blessed Virgin, it wasn't one of my sons? Tell me it wasn't one of my sons," Bess implored, shaking her.

A voice from behind said, "It was me, Mother. It was me."

She turned around to see Moses standing there, holding his ground like a towering oak tree. Lénaïg smiled at him.

"Oh, you fool. What will my Lady Margaret say?" implored Bess. "You can't acknowledge the birth. We shall have to marry Lénaïg off."

"My Lady Margaret can say what she likes," said Moses firmly. "Lénaïg stays here and I acknowledge the child as mine."

Moses took Lénaïg by the hand and led her out to the byre. She had contained her emotions for months but now the built-up tension was released she looked uncharacteristically vulnerable. Moses thought she looked like some little fawn he had burst upon in the woods, its heart pounding and its flanks shaking, with those big pleading doe-like eyes. He smiled and kissed her on top of the head, breathing in the scent of her hair.

"Be not afraid, none will do you any harm. You are the mother of my child. They will have me to answer to," he soothed.

Lénaïg smiled at him through tears that she could no longer contain.

"I could not bear to be parted from you, ever. I was afraid they'd marry me off to some stinking peasant in a hovel. I could not lay down with someone like that. All I have ever known is you. All I ever want is you. And now we are to have a child," she beamed.

"Aye, we are to have a child," said Moses poignantly, "but you know we can never be married. They will not allow that as long as there is a chance of me inheriting my estates."

"That might never happen," suggested Lénaïg hopefully.

"Maybe," replied Tom wistfully, "but where there is life there is hope. Nothing we can do about that now, though. The boy will have my name on the parish register; he will know who his father is."

"Boy, how do you know it will be a boy?" laughed Lénaïg.

"Because we Cliffords are of virile stock and only produce tups, speaking of which…" and he grabbed her round the waist with one arm, the other fondling her buttocks, easing her gently into the hay while she screamed and giggled and wriggled and writhed on their makeshift bed.

To his wife's dismay, Tom Lawkland was pleased at the news.

"Always something to celebrate when a newborn bairn comes into the world. Hey, and I'll be a grandfatha too," he beamed. Ralph and Luke took every opportunity to rib their brother about his promiscuity but were careful not to say anything in front of Lénaïg for fear of upsetting her, and also for fear of her fiery temper. It was light-hearted banter though, and Moses felt secretly proud of his accomplishment and was openly protective of his lover.

When the child was born, Moses named him Anthony, but thereafter, Tom always referred to him as Rufus on account of his red hair. He was a lusty young babe and soon grew into a sturdy young version of his father, strutting around the Hall like he owned the place. He was devoted to Moses and he to Anthony, and the family were glad to see such joy in their midst.

In truth, all concerned would have been happy for things to continue this way, but it was not to be. The world of Moses, Lord Henry Clifford, was about to be turned on its head again.

CHAPTER 23

THE HEAVENS SPOKE

S O IT WAS THE NIGHT OF THE twelfth of August, 1485, that Tom Lawkland came to visit Moses up on his summer shieling. The previous summers had been wet and cloudy, not unusual for that part of the world, but this summer was different. A dry July and August made it easy for them to scythe and dry out the hay on the mountain meadows, and the harvest was good.

Moses' star-gazing had been aided by the clear night skies and this made him particularly reflective. The night was still and silent and even the screech owls and foxes were quiet. The air was full of static. It was as if the world had just begun. He was deep in thought when Tom broke the silence.

"Is summat on tha' mind, son?" he asked, leaning forward.

Moses looked at him but merely shook his head, saying nothing.

"Cause if there's summat that's worrying thee, tha' can allus tell me."

Moses looked at him again and said, "I don't really know, Fatha. I've everything to be happy for but I just feel a bit strange. I can't put me finger on it but I've this feeling. Does tha' ever get same? When tha' feels summat's going to happen but tha' doesn't know what it is?"

Tom scratched his head. "Sometimes, I gets like that afore a storm. There are no signs in sky or 'owt but I just knows that one's brewing. Does tha' mean summat like that?"

Moses didn't reply. He was staring at the sky in a trance-like state, craning his neck to the heavens and trembling, mumbling to himself.

Tom tried to shake him gently by the shoulder but it was to no avail. Then he saw what was distracting Moses – a spectacular sight, filling him with awe. A meteor shower tore across the sky in a myriad of colours. Long-haired stars with tails of flame illuminating the fellside and picking out the profile of the contours and jagged rocks.

The two men stood transfixed. Long after the shower disappeared over the ridge of Whernside they stayed rooted to the spot as if held by some magic spell.

Tom eventually shook his head and said, "By the blessed Virgin, in all my born days I've never seen…" but Moses interrupted him, grabbing him by the arm, looking grim-faced and determined.

"That was it, Fatha. The sign I have been waiting for. My Heavenly Father has spoken to me. This is the sign I was waiting for. A great portent. Go and tell Lady Margaret I intend to declare my birthright. I will go home and make ready for my journey, hence the way we came. I want you, I *need* thee, to come with me," and with this he gripped Tom tighter by the arm and looked earnestly into his eyes.

***

Elsewhere, the seer looked closely into the eyes of Richard III.

"Sire, I tell thee. This does not bode well for the House of York. The trailing meteor foretells the decline of the noble Plantagenet line. Your symbol of a white rose, emblazoned with the golden rays of the ascending sun, is dashing to the ground as we speak."

"Nonsense," snapped Richard, "it's just the Perseids,[25] a natural phenomenon that happens every year. The only difference is that this year it's visible in the heavens as there are no clouds obscuring the view. And to think I pay you for this. What would you have me do, anyway? Run away like a scared girl and give up my throne to that slimy Welsh bastard? I will die first. And if I do, I'll die as a true King."

Despite Richard's words, what was undeniable was the sad fact that the Richard of August 1485 was not the hopeful, optimistic Richard of July 1483 by any means. By that fateful summer, he was beleaguered

---

25. As with spectacular storms and winds, whenever a comet appears, it is bound to portend great events. Tacitus thought so, and Bede in the Eighth Century agreed – 'Comets are long-haired stars with flames, appearing suddenly, and presaging a change in sovereignty, or plague, or war, or winds, or floods' (De Natura Rerum).

as well as betrayed and bereaved. His son and his wife had died, leaving no natural heir to the throne, and although he was young enough to have other sons, the longer he waited, the longer England had to foment and ponder over the succession. Whilst there was no obvious heir, the kingdom was unstable.

The young princes, sons of his brother, Edward IV, had been sent away into hiding – the eldest to Ireland and the youngest to the North Country. He might have been confident and unconcerned about his own safety, but he would not risk the lives of his nephews. Their lives were too precious to him and there had been enough blood spilt. No, if there was any blood to be spilt, it would be that of the leek-eating, deformed Welsh scumbag, Henry Tudor. Why, the bastard had written to potential supporters in England while he was skulking in his hiding place in Brittany, where he was attended by young Richard Clifford and other exiles. He had condemned Richard as a 'homicide and an unabated tyrant', and signed himself, H.R. Henricus Rex. He would choke on that bloody name, Richard would see to it.

As the young princes had not been seen in public for a while, Henry put it about that Richard had smothered the young lads in their sleep. This rumour was swiftly quashed but there was no escaping the fact that Richard was without an heir and without a wife to produce another one. These events gave many in the kingdom the conviction that Richard was an unlucky King and that God had deserted him.

He had tried to bribe Brittany's corrupt Treasurer, Pierre Landau, to surrender Henry Tudor to him and all was going well until someone foiled the plot. That someone was Margaret Beaufort, who was told the news by her husband, Lord Thomas Stanley, a supposedly loyal supporter of the King.

Margaret Beaufort was first married to the Earl of Richmond and the wedding took place when she was only twelve years old, the earliest legal age for sexual intercourse. From this union sprang Henry Tudor. It was a traumatic experience for her as she was still physically immature, and she bore no children again. She did marry a second time, though, and her next husband was a Stanley, Lord Thomas Stanley, steward to Richard's brother, Edward IV. Thomas was elder brother to Sir William Stanley and every inch as sycophantic and untrustworthy.

Richard, a true man of action, could not wait for events and paid little heed to politics. He raised an army in readiness. When the news broke that Henry Tudor had landed at Milford Haven, he rejoiced at the opportunity of taking on such a contemptible enemy. He was heavily reliant on the Earl of Northumberland, the Duke of Norfolk and the Stanleys, though. He was a shrewd King, and had a sneaking feeling about the turncoat Stanleys. He took Lord Strange, son of Lord Thomas Stanley, as a hostage. Let the slimy brothers, Thomas and William, thwart him now.

CHAPTER 24

BOSWORTH

LORD WILLIAM STANLEY SAT SMILING ASTRIDE HIS charger, at the flank of Richard III's hastily assembled army at Bosworth. Henry Tudor, since landing at Milford Haven with his French and Breton mercenaries, had raised a formidable army, but Richard's still outnumbered them if he could just rely on the Stanleys. Thomas Stanley had prevaricated by pleading illness, no doubt shitting his pants, thought Richard, but William had men enough to tip the balance. Surely he would not dare risk his nephew's life as hostage, or so gambled Richard.

Richard was the more experienced soldier and practised every day with the sword. Whilst slim of frame he possessed a wiry strength and his sword arm bulged with sinewy muscle. He was particularly adept at battering through his opponents with a swirling battle-axe and his men laughingly called him a berserker.

Henry was untested in battle and although his subordinate commander, the Earl of Oxford, was no slouch as a general, the odds were stacked in Richard's favour. If the King waited long enough, his troops would swell to 12,000 whilst Henry's numbered only 5,000. What he really needed was the support of the Stanleys, but who knew which side they would take? He had one of their number as hostage, he had parleyed with them before the battle and they had made all the right noises, but their word was no more reliable than that of a drunken Welsh pedlar.

Richard had positioned himself well on the high ground of Ambien Hill, facing west, watching with interest the advance of the upstart's army. The Duke of Norfolk took up Richard's defences, fanning out a stout column with artillery on either side. Behind them were the King's main guard and at the rear, the Earl of Northumberland, ready to reinforce either flank. All they had to do was stand firm and the day would be theirs. A victory fought on solid defence was not good enough for Richard, though. He wanted to engage Henry in mortal combat. He wanted to cut swathes through the Lancastrian force and call out the cringing coward. Who would act like the King on the day?

Henry and Oxford made the first move. They had no choice. The longer the day went on, the more reinforcements would arrive for Richard. That was plain enough.

Yorkist archers fired on the Lancastrian army and the hail of arrows made heavy casualties. Oxford shortened his line to minimize the target and make the archers work harder for their kill. When the Yorkist men-at-arms engaged, it was into a compact Lancastrian force that was hard to repel due to the depth of the re-formed column. Blood-spattered men screamed and there was an overriding stench of blood, fear and shit in the air. The men hacked at each other and the foremost troops were so pressed into the fray by their own troops, eager to get to the front, that many were crushed and suffocated in the melee. As there was to be no decisive result from this encounter, the Yorkists pulled back to regroup. Whilst this was a good tactical move, and in no way disadvantaged his troops, it irritated Richard. A Plantagenet does not walk backwards, he said to himself.

Anxiously, Richard looked to the north, where Stanley was watching with his troops. His flank was weakened. If he was to win this battle, nay keep his crown, he needed Stanley to act now. He needed him to commit his troops. The sweat was pouring down his brow, stinging his eyes and making the view from his visor more obscured than ever. What was the man doing? Didn't he know how to soldier? Was he craven?

Sir William Stanley surveyed the field. He pondered awhile. If he committed his men to the Yorkist attack, he would save the day for the King. Richard, however, was unlikely to forgive him for being so uncommitted, and certainly not his brother for staying at home. If he helped Henry, however, the day would be lost. Lost for Richard that was, but not for Stanley, as he could claim even greater reward from Henry Tudor, as had been agreed by secret parley.

It was then that reality dawned on Richard, this firebrand head of the House of York. The treacherous Stanley was not going to commit until he saw which side had the upper hand. Richard's staff counselled withdrawal. At that very moment, Henry Tudor, also uncertain of the outcome, left the main body of his army and advanced towards Lord Stanley to appeal to him in person.

Upon seeing this, Richard was furious and made a charge against Henry's smaller band of horsemen. He was livid with rage but he also realized that his superiority in numbers should smash through the Lancastrian formation. He noticed a gap opening up between Oxford's right flank, away from the marshy ground. His heavy cavalry carved a large opening through the enemy lines, scattering soldiers this way and that, some foundering in the marsh. And he had the advantage of surprise. The King and his household hacked down Henry's small bodyguard of knights and Richard himself, with heaving chest and blood pounding in his ears, killed Henry's standard-bearer, Sir William Brandon. But at the moment Richard was within sight of Tudor, Stanley threw caution to the wind and, taking the more lucrative of the choices on hand, came to Henry's rescue.

Richard soon realized what was happening. He railed across the battle-field, "You traitorous bastard, Stanley! A pox on your slimy family for all eternity! I smear shite on your name and will see you in hell!" and with this he spurred his horse against these new adversaries.

The traitors threw themselves into the fray against the smaller York-ist bodyguard, overwhelming them. Richard had the fighting fury in him, though, and none dared get too close for fear of his swirling sword arm and the relentless slicing of his great battle-axe. In the struggle, Richard's own standard-bearer had both of his legs hewn away. Such was his loyalty that he did not let the banner fall, but instead held on to it until he was finally put to death by a band of Stanley's fearful soldiers.

At the sight of this, Richard redoubled his efforts and fought like a King should. His charger was hacked from under him but he regained his footing long enough to batter two opponents to their knees with his war axe. He was heaving with exertion but he was not going to sell his life cheaply. He saw Stanley's liveried surcoat and cut swathes through men-at-arms and the slippery blood of the battlefield to reach him. Stanley raised his visor and Richard could see fear in his eyes. He shouted, "En garde, Stanley, I may lose my life on this day but I swear by all that is true to me that you will perish too."

This was not to be, for poor Richard was cruelly poleaxed from behind by a foot soldier. Only when he dropped to his knees did Stanley make his move and hack at Richard's dying body with his sword.

Henry quickly came to the scene and said, "Today you have killed a King and made one of me." He looked at Lord Stanley's fawning face and declared, "The King is ever in your debt. Right well have you served me and right well will I serve you."

Stanley spied the fallen King Richard's crown circlet tangled in a bush and retrieved it. He slyly placed the bloody circlet on Tudor's helmet and said, "And now, there is no doubt, Sire. Here is your crown and you are anointed with Yorkist blood." And all the while the ravens circled overhead.

All who saw him die agreed that Richard had fought bravely to the end, but this did not prevent the Welsh billmen stripping off his armour, bartering his weapons and dumping his blood-spattered body into the marshy ground, spitting on the corpse. Later, the body was unceremoniously strapped to a broken-winded pack horse and taken to Newark where it was callously displayed for two days to prove that the King was truly dead. Only Henry's cronies rejoiced. The rest of the nation was stunned. When would the bloodshed stop?

And this was how it came to pass that Richard became the last of the Plantagenets and the last English King to die on the battlefield.

CHAPTER 25

TRISTRAM BOLLING

A knight that for a lion fought,
Against a herd of bears.
Was to lang toil and trouble brought,
In which some thousands shares.
But now again the lion rares,
And joy spreads o'er the plain:
The lion has defeat the bears,
The knight returns again.

The knight, in a few days, shall bring
A shepherd frae the fauld,
And shall present him to his King,
A subject true and bauld.

The Gentle Shepherd
Allan Ramsay

TRISTRAM BOLLING SAT IN THE BANQUETING HALL, a lone figure, waiting anxiously for his midday meal well before the arrival of the rest of his household. Today, the meal was perch, his favourite, and he could not abide the dish going cold. His appearance had changed somewhat since he had delivered the news of the defeat at Towton to Lady Margaret as a youth. He had kept his swarthy good looks, although his figure had filled out now; he was much broader in the shoulder and had the look of a soldier about him. Only the grey hair in his temples belied his age but that only served to give him a distinguished look.

124

His wife, brothers, daughter and servants arrived noisily and a serving maid moved the settle so that they could all reach the table comfortably before sitting down, servants and masters alike.

"Ah, Beatrice," he said, "I wondered what was keeping you?" He pronounced her name Beer-triss, like in beer the drink, and she winced.

"*Bear*-treece," she corrected him. "Like in the animal, the bear. How often do I have to remind you, my husband?"

"Yes, Beer-triss," he replied in his strong Yorkshire accent.

Everyone laughed but the jesting ceased when a grey-faced steward entered the hall.

"There is a messenger outside for you, My Lord. He says he will speak with none but you. I offered to box his ears for his insolence but he is adamant that he must speak with you alone. He says it is a matter of national importance."

"Send him in," instructed Tristram. "Let's have a look at the colour of his eyes."

The messenger, a well-dressed and clean limbed young man, entered the hall and looked nervously about him.

"Well?" bellowed Tristram. "What have you got to say for yourself, young fellow?"

The young man coughed to clear his throat and said, "It is a matter for your ears only, My Lord. I have promised to deliver it to no one but you. I mean to cause no offence to the good people in your household, but is there somewhere more private we can talk?"

"We can talk in a while, after I am assured that you mean me no harm. Search him first, look for signs of concealed weapons or poison," he asked of his brothers. Humphrey and Rainbrow flanked the nervous messenger on either side and roughly frisked him for any signs of concealed weapons. The young man stood still with arms out open, looking steadfastly at Tristram all the time.

Rainbrow looked across and said, "Nothing but the parchment in his hand. Here, let me have a look at that to make sure you have no stiletto concealed inside. The young man instinctively clutched the parchment to his chest but Rainbrow was strong and he grabbed him by the wrist. The messenger held on to the parchment but something heavy fell on the floor.

Tristram looked on astounded. His face coloured and he was breathless. There, lying on the floor, was the black and white pendant from a horse harness, bearing his coat of arms. The one he had given to Lady Margaret at Skipton.

"Leave the boy be!" he bellowed. "He means me no harm. Oh my Lady, my lady, after all these years you have come to me."

He moved quickly round the table and scooped the pendant up, concealing it in his fist. He took the boy by the arm and led him into the wooden passageway betwixt the banqueting hall and the kitchen. When he broke the seal, all that was written on the document were the words, Brough Castle, but also inside the parchment roll was a single red rose.

He staggered back into the hall, clutching the red rose and looking at the pendant whilst shaking his head.

His daughter, Rosamund, asked, "When are we going to eat, Father?" but all thoughts of food had left his head.

"Send for my armour. Send for my sword and buckler. Saddle my war horse," he demanded of the steward. "Make sure this young boy is fed and given wine before we go on our journey."

This was too much for Beatrice. Despite her normal calm demeanour she could not help but burst into floods of tears.

This broke Tristram from his reverie. "Why, whatever is the matter, my love?" he cooed. He was truly fond of his wife and hated to see her in distress.

"Don't you profess love to me, you false cur. You have taken another love and leave me now to be by her side. How do you explain that rose you are holding fondly to your bosom?"

At first the words stung Tristram, but then, when he realized how things must seem, he laughed. He laughed a deep, side-splitting, wheezing belly laugh that soon saw tears streaming down his cheeks. His brothers looked on in astonishment and his daughter ran to his side, clutching his hand, nestling her face into his doublet. He stroked her hair and tried to control his laughter.

"Another lover? Another lover? You think I treat you false?" he demanded.

"Look how it must seem, brother," interrupted Rainbrow. "A mystery messenger and a red rose…"

"Aye, a red rose. A red rose all right. A red rose of the House of Lancaster. How many times have I told you the story? Did you think it was idle boasting? Look, here, the Bolling coat of arms from my horse harness. The horse I took to Towton. This is the token I gave to my Lady Margaret at Skipton the day after the battle. A token to show my loyalty to the Cliffords and all that serve the House of Lancaster. She has returned it and needs my help."

Tristram's family and servants crowded round and jostled each other to see the beautifully crafted Limoges pendant in the outstretched palm of his hand.

Beatrice's lips were still trembling. "Please, my husband; do not put yourself in danger. I fear for your life on this enterprise and, remember, it took your father full fourteen years to have our lands restored the last time you bore arms."

"Danger? Danger? I have old scores to settle. I will unfurl the red rose banner and see justice for all those brave men who were butchered at Towton. It is high time this county knows who their rightful rulers are. The usurper lies dead and my lady Margaret has an errand for me, I'll be bound. Humphrey, you are to look after my affairs whilst I am gone and make sure that Rainbrow does not get up to his tricks. I am still paying for his misdemeanours from the last time I was away."

And with the first jaunty step for many years, Tristram was away to the stables on his adventure.

He travelled with only one servant, Harold, a big solid man and a skilled archer. They rode with great speed, stopping overnight only once, more for the sake of resting their horses rather than themselves.

Lady Margaret looked down from the turret of Brough Castle as Tristram and his companion approached. She saw the black and white livery of the Bollings on horse and rider, and her mind tunnelled back to that fateful day, more than twenty years ago, when the same young man brought her news of the death of her husband. Her heart still raced at the thought of John Clifford. In truth, she had never stopped loving him, even though she had remarried and the grief of his sudden departure had never left her. He had been such an attentive, kind and caring man, and those base people, less worthy than he, had sought to besmirch his good name. Well, his image was beside her now. A strapping brute of a man, who was going to restore the good name of the Cliffords. This had been her life's work. Her one desire and nothing was going to get in the way of success.

The iron horseshoes of Tristram's mount sparked on the cobbles of Brough Castle, just like they had at Skipton all those years ago. He dismounted but this time he looked at her more ruefully and approached slowly, bowing low and kissing her hand.

She smiled, not trying to hide the tears that were welling in her eyes and said, "I called and you came. Just like I knew you would. Loyal as ever. I can never forget the earnest young man that came and told me that fateful news on that day, and you, hardly more than a boy. You will ever be the knight errant in my heart."

At this Tristram blushed and bowed more deeply.

"Come, I have someone I want you to meet. Someone who is in need of you," she smiled. She took Tristram by the hand and led him to a shaded corner of the courtyard.

"Come out now, Henry," she called. Out of the shadows a large man appeared standing in the full sunlight, its rays setting the blond flecks in his hair and beard ablaze with a radiant halo.

Tristram stood there dumbfounded, his mouth working and his hand hanging loosely by his side while his brain fathomed what was happening.

"It can't be," he said. "It can't be. The son and heir of My Lord Clifford. Where have you been hiding all these years past?"

"With me," said a voice from the shadows and another figure emerged, carrying a large crosier staff.

"I's brought lad up wi' me, as me own bairn. Best shepherd I ever had. It's a shame to lose him but it can't be helped. I allus knew it would come to this one day," said Tom Lawkland with bitter irony.

Henry laughed and pushed the man playfully on the shoulder whilst Tristram exclaimed, "The Shepherd Lord. That's what you are. The Shepherd Lord. The seed that has grown from the bitter tomb of Towton. By the Blessed Virgin, all I see before me is a miracle."

"That is precisely how I thought you would take it," said Lady Margaret, smiling now at Tristram's reaction. "I would ask that you help present Henry at court to the new king. We must play this very skilfully as there are those that will suffer from his restoration. We must play a very strong suit. I have chosen you for your wisdom and insight and your standing in the County.

Your family have an even older affinity with the shire than the Cliffords. We must show our new sovereign that Henry has the support of the North Country people. Come inside and let us talk some more."

Assembled together in the withdrawing room, Tristram warmed to his task. "Symbolism. That's what it's all about these days – symbolism. We must decide what represents the North Country best, and that way, demonstrate to His Royal Majesty Henry VII that we embody all that is wholesome in these lands. That we will rule by the will of the common people and that there will be no unrest. We need to show him that we epitomize strength and will protect his borders against those treacherous Scots. He needs to know that we will make the area rich again and produce lots of fleeces to sell to Flanders, all the more that he might levy taxes. Above all, we need an iconic figure that will replace that usurper, Richard, in the hearts of the people. That man was too much the peasant's lackey in my opinion."

"And how do you propose we do this?" asked Lady Margaret, smiling encouragingly at Tristram's great enthusiasm.

"Why, we have a story that is straight out of the bible. The good shepherd, chased into hiding by the forces of darkness, but blossoming in the nurture of our North Country fells. The devil's helpers tried to kill the poor innocent at Londesborough and then at Threlkeld but the Good Lord's angels were watching over him and the Yorkists got their comeuppance! Raised by simple folk," he said, nodding with deference to Tom, "but the noble blood of the Cliffords will out. The flower of the ancient House of Cliffords growing from the twisted wreck of Towton. Folk like nothing more than a good tale and this is a better one than Robin of the Hood."

"But symbolism," said Lady Margaret; "you said symbolism."

"Yes, and lots of it," enthused Tristram. "The symbol of the lamb and the flag. St John, the Patron Saint of Shepherds. Am I right, Master Lawkland?"

"Aye," intoned Tom, looking bemused at all the proceedings.

"And we will have flags all right. I will lead with a Bolling pennant, showing you have the support of the gentry, and my Lord Henry's men will follow with a pennant with the Clifford arms and another with the red rose of Lancaster. As for the lamb, we'll take a big ram to show them our strength and virility. Yon fellow there can pick his biggest and best and follow on with his staff. And just look at those dogs. Did you ever see such dogs? We'll take three of those mastiffs and have those collies flanking us. That will show them what we are about. We protect our own in Yorkshire. And archers, we must have archers dressed in Lincoln Green. They must be hand picked. Every one of them over six foot. England is protected by archers – our enemies fear their straight arrow shafts. And as for you, My Lord, you will need a tailor to dress you in the latest court fashion."

Henry remained silent while all of this discourse was going on. He looked distinctly uncomfortable. When Tristram had finished and was waiting for everyone to acclaim his ideas, Henry turned to Tom and said, "I can't do it, Fatha. I can't do as he says with all that fuss. When all is said and done, I'm a simple shepherd and have never been to London. I know I won't like it and I won't hold me own with all them fancy folk."

Tom gripped him by the arm and looked squarely into his eyes.

"Tha'll do it all right or tha's not the son that I knows. I've raised thee to never shy away from tha' duties and tha's nivver let me down. How does tha' know tha' can't do it until tha' tries? Me and thee mother are right proud of thee and have been waiting for this day. Tha' can show folk that we've raised thee good and proper. Do it, our Mo, do it for me. As long as tha' tries tha' best, I don't mind. If tha' dares to try and fails, at least tha's dared to try and that's the mark of the man."

Henry, all the while returning his gaze, smiled through tears. Tristram was surprised to see this huge bear of a man show such emotion.

At last Henry spoke. "I'll do it, Fatha. I'll do it as long as tha's with me."

"I'll be with thee, son. I won't let thee down," said Tom, "and I knows tha'll put on a good show. Just be thysen and act like tha' allus does. Any true man in this kingdom would be proud to name thee as his friend and look up to thee as a Lord."

Tristram looked at Tom with new respect. This was no ordinary man.

Margaret sniffed and said, "And now, my son, you must learn how to write your name. You can't sign the King's treaties with the mark of a cross!"

CHAPTER 26

TOM LAWKLAND -
THE COURT OF HENRY TUDOR
AT WESTMINSTER

I REARED A SHEEPDOG ON THE SUMMER pastures, high up on the fells one year. It was a magnificent animal. When I brought it down the mountain, no matter how I bid it, it wouldn't enter the house. So, I tricked it and made it walk in backwards. When it realized where it was, it looked as if it had walked straight into a trap. It dug its nails into the floor in sheer horror, staring in terror at the windows, yelping at the walls and howling at the hearth and all that surrounded it. All it had known was the fells and I suppose, we're all in fear of the unknown – just like it was in that house.

That's how I felt when I went to Henry Tudor's court. I'm an outdoors person, tha' knows, more suited to big skies and open spaces. Me? To be in the presence of the King? If anyone had ever said I'd be at court with the King of England, why I'd strike him on the pate for being a fool. But I had to go, for the sake of our Moses, or Henry as we now must call him. He was getting to look more like a Henry. His mother had trimmed his hair and beard and gotten him some fine clothes. He weren't comfortable wearing them but she made him stick at it. He were right worried about being presented at court and I knew how he felt but there was no way round it. I thought a lot about it. The trick was to show no fear and act like there was nothing to it, even though your insides have turned to liquid. That's how the nobles behaved. I'd a new-found respect for Lady Margaret. All that time our lad was in hiding, she'd had to put a brave face on it.

131

Henry, he were that worried he'd seem a gawk to others, but me and that Tristram fellow, we put him straight. There was no point him trying to talk fancy. It wouldn't have suited him for he was a big, rough man now, bigger than me. Tristram said how this would add to his air of mystery. I said to him, "Act like tha's been brought up to do. Tha's one of nature's gentlemen. And don't let anyone get the better of thee. If any fellow does thee a mischief, pay him back double. There'll be none of them at court that can fill out a suit of clothes like thee and tha' mother's got thee dressed up like a peacock. Tha' fatha would be right proud to see thee thus. And don't forget, I'll be there for thee, just like I've allus been."

Well, he seemed to get more confidence day by day. Like I explained to him, this was a job just like shepherding and, like any other job, tha'd to practice and work hard at it.

That Tristram fellow, he told him what to expect. He made him practise his entrance, made us all practise what he called the grand entrance. To pause, hold our breath, take a long look at everyone else and give them time to take us all in. Make some impact, he kept saying. Well, if that's how we were supposed to act, who was I to gainsay him? Let's just get on wi' job and get it out of road. The sooner we got back to Yorkshire, the better it suited me.

I've never seen the likes of London and I don't care if I ever see it again. I've been to York and I've been to Beverley but I never expected anything like this. The sounds were deafening, folk talking all at once and some of them foreigners. The smells were disgusting. It's not natural to have folk and beasts crowded into one place like that. And the people? All crowding round trying to jostle thee and sell thee things tha'd no need of. Tristram, he'd the hang of it. He'd raise his riding crop to anyone who came close, so we all followed suit. Our Henry, he set dogs on a few of them and they soon learned to make way for us. We cut a swathe right through them and they all looked on in wonder, for I reckon they'd never seen a sight like us.

The court of Henry Tudor. That were summat else. If folk want to spend all their money on things like that, I suppose it's up to them, but I can think of better ways to spend my silver. No rushes on the floor, tiles mind you, from Italy or somewhere like that. Wall hangings from Flanders and pictures on the wall. A gurt big hall. So big that I can hardly describe it to thee. I felt like I were going into a big cavern under fells. All I could do was stare up at the ceiling with its massive hammer beams. There was an oak forest up there.

When we entered, everyone went silent. Just stared at us. We did as Tristram had said. Stopped stark still, and let 'em all take a good look at us. They stared at us open mouthed. King, he wasn't there, he were in his private chambers, but there were some mighty lords and ladies there and they just gawped.

On the nod from Tristram, we made our grand entrance. Dogs went first. The King's greyhounds – wonderful white beasts with red studded collars – they made to attack our Henry's dogs but one snarl from the mastiffs had them cowering in the corner. Then Tristram went next, swaggering around like he owned the place, nodding to this one and that. Flanked by the collies, he were. I had to whistle to keep 'em in check, some close field work that day I can tell thee.

Then, our archers, some carrying the pennants of Bolling, Clifford and the red rose of Lancaster, but most with their bows strung, carried on their right side. The yew wood oiled and polished like prized jewels. Every one of them decked out the same in Lincoln Green and all the size of a barn doorway. They moved in unison, like Tristram had schooled them, and were a real sight to behold.

Next, it were me, leading Jacob, our prize tup, on a studded leather leash. Staff in hand, me best one, a twisting shaft fashioned wi' a big ramshorn crosier that had taken me all of one winter to shape and polish. I'd to wear a big sheepskin cloak made from four curly fleeced yaws. It was still summer but I'd to wear it for effect, Tristram said.

Last of all was Henry. His mother had him fitted up in the latest fashion. He wore a blue cap in the Italian style, rather than a chaperon, and it had the biggest sapphire jewel in it you'd ever seen. And a silver and black suit that showed off his great frame and broad shoulders with a ruff at the collar. His shoes were broad, not pointed in the English way, and he looked every inch the fine gentleman. And he were smiling. Smiling fit to burst. I thought he'd taken a funny turn but then I saw why he was smiling. There, in King Henry's court, was the Nut-Brown Maid. By all the blessed saints, she was a beauty and she was smiling right back at him, which set all the other ladies gossiping. One checked me, and asked, "Who is that fine lord?"

"The Lord's my shepherd," I said truthfully, and I never was more proud of him than on that day. Holding his own with all the greatest in the land and it were me that had raised him. She rushed over to a group of ladies to tell 'em but I could see by the looks on theirs faces they didn't believe her.

As we passed toward the King's chamber, someone made a bleating noise. Everyone thought it were right funny and laughed. Our Henry, he just stops and turns round, looking everyone in the face. Then he stops at one of 'em, a funny looking little bugger, as he was the one that had blushed when our Henry looked him in the eye. He walks over to him and by this time the fellow's face was in high colour. Our Henry, he could move quick for a big man, and he cupped his shovel of a right hand round this fellow's neck, bowing it to his knees whilst putting his left arm under the fellow's waist, heaving him, arse first, into the air.

"Here's a little lamb as needs dagging," he says, placing the flat of his dagger on the fellow's plump buttocks. "Or maybe I should make him into a wether?"

Everyone's laughing even more now at the discomfort of the little fool and our Henry smiles back and gently sets the fellow down on to his feet.

He wasn't going to be happy about this. No one would, but his temper got the better of him and he drew his sword. Henry looked over to me and I knew what I must do. I threw my staff across to him and he caught it dead easy and knocked the sword out of the little bugger's hand in one swift movement. Knocked him right on the fist and he yelped and let go the sword, which arced high into the air for our Henry to catch it. He then presented the blade to the fellow, hilt-first and said, "My cousin D'Acre, I'm right glad to see thee after all these years. How is thee mother?"

The fellow just gawped at him like a landed carp and our Henry; he just smiles and walks on. I'll tell thee, no one else made to bleat like a sheep that day.

Then it was Henry's turn to be surprised, for out of the shadows stepped his brother, Richard. A slimmer, paler version of Henry with more delicate features, but there was no mistaking they were brothers. They stood staring at each other for a while before embracing. Richard said, after leaving England, he had made for Henry Tudor's court in exile in Brittany or some such foreign place, and had pledged his allegiance.

The two lads had so much to talk about but this was not the time. It was then that Tristram came into his own. He borrows my staff and bangs it thrice on the floor until he has everyone's attention. He then tells them all such a story about how our Henry was spirited away after Towton and hidden away for fear of his life. How the Yorkies had sent the evil assassin, Eldroth, and how I had killed him with me bare hands. How we had fled to Westmorland and lived amongst wolves, bears, wildcats, murdering Scotsmen and a gurt barguest[26] with red eyes that roamed the misty moors at night. He held them all in thrall. Even the King's guards moved from their post by his chamber door to listen. I was very nearly spellbound with it too, and I only recognized but half of it as truth.

Then he tells of treacherous Lord Stanley and how he had sent a full company of soldiers to kill our Henry and how's the lad had a guardian angel at his side who hurled huge, jagged boulders down from the mountain and smote them all dead. Everyone gasps and looks toward a fat old beggar with shifty eyes and Tristram points at him long and hard.

"That," he says, "that creature is a traitor most foul. A murderer of innocent babes, a turncoat and an enemy of the King. Arrest him!"

Well, the King's guards, they looks at each other not knowing quite what to do. Lord Stanley, he thinks it's time to say fare-thee-well and makes for the door, but I weren't about to let the bugger who tried to kill our Henry get away. Two whistles and I has the mastiffs pinning him against wall. He blusters and pleads his innocence, saying how it was all lies but no one believes him, and even his shifty friends turn their backs on him.

"You see how the Shepherd Lord has prevailed," says Tristram. "How the blood of the Cliffords runs strong through his veins. He has come to claim his birthright and denounce that wicked villain, Stanley, oppressor

---

26. A spectral hound that was reputed to roam the moors.

of the poor and evil necromancer."

Our Henry says, in a calm voice, how it's time to see the King, but curiosity had got the better of His Majesty, for he comes out of his chambers to see what all the fuss was about.

He were a right odd fish if you ask me, eyes that looked at you like a rat peering through a corn sheath and a miserly, thin-lipped smile. I've spoken to a few who knew the last King, Richard, and said what a proper fellow he was. What kind pale blue eyes he had, a proper King as cared for folk. But, everyone bows to this fellow right enough, then he asks his guards to take Stanley away to the Tower so's he could explain himsen at His Majesty's pleasure.

I knows I shouldn't, I knows I spoke out of turn, but I couldn't help myself and I shouted out as they were leading him away, "Aye, and when yon King's finished with thee, I'll be having a word an' all, Yitney."[27]

There was a deathly silence, but Tristram, he broke it by bursting out laughing and saying what loyal subjects His Majesty had, and soon the King and everyone else is laughing too. Then Henry Tudor takes our Henry by the arm and leads him away to his private chambers for a parley.

Tristram come across to me and winks. "Strike while the iron's hot as the good blacksmith says."

I looks at him, old-fashioned like.

"Your charge, young Henry Clifford, can ask what he wants of the King," he says. "He'll get it. Henry Tudor needs friends in the north. There'll be trouble fomenting after the death of Richard and he needs someone to distract them from their grievances. The other lords are too ambitious and vying for power so he'll grant young Clifford vast estates to balance that power, and what better talisman do the common people have than the Shepherd Lord? They'll respect someone who's toiled in the field alongside them and shared their troubles. What's more, good friend, we'll have Stanley sent back to whence he came and, no doubt, His Majesty will take kindly to the Bollings and grant me some of the old trout's lands and offices. What is it you say? Never do 'owt for nowt."

He winked again but stopped to cup his ear as the guards shouted for

---

27. Literally a cowardly fellow in Yorkshire dialect.

Ann St John to attend the King.

"That's the King's cousin," he says, but when I looked it were the Nut Brown Maid.

Well, our Henry is in there for ages and I'm getting bored. All these folk stood round idle at court and doing nowt but gossip. I'd soon find 'em work to do on the fells.

Finally, our Henry comes out with a daft grin on his face. He beckons for us to follow him out of the hall but says nowt. Not until we're outside, that is, and he punches me on the arm. "I've done it, Fatha," he says. "I've got the King to give me the hand of Ann St John in marriage. I'm to be Lord Henry Clifford and she is to be my lady."

"I'm right pleased for thee, lad," I says. "And what a fitting name."

"What does tha' mean, Fatha?" he says.

"Ann St John. St John the Baptist is the patron saint of shepherds and you, you are the Shepherd Lord."

CHAPTER 27

HENRY CLIFFORD -
10TH LORD OF SKIPTON

Ye shall not nede further to drede:
I will not disparàge
You (God defend), sith you descend
Of so great a linàge.
Now understand: to Westmoreland,
Which is my heritage,
I will you bring; and with a ring,
By way of marriàge
I will you take, and lady make,
As shortly as I can:
Thus have you won an Earles son,
And not a banished man.

The Nut Brown Maid
Poem Anon

HENRY, LORD OF THE HONOUR OF SKIPTON, Westmorland and Vipont, was a celebrity in his time, much more so as the citizens of London were granted a feast day by the King, in his honour. There was much talk about his exploits, fuelled by strong drink and encouraged by first-hand accounts from Tristram. He was called upon to demonstrate his prowess with a staff and explained how he had many years of practice, brought about by the boredom of long winter nights and the necessity of defending himself, always with the prospect of vengeful Yorkists hunting him down, nagging at the back of his mind.

Some went as far as adopting the shepherd look with a fleece collar on their cloaks as a new fashion, and for a while the humble sheepdog took precedence over hunting dogs in many a household.

Henry's priority was his wedding preparations, though, and he could not wait to return back to the north to Skipton Castle. It had to be there as he somehow felt he still had to prove to his Nut Brown Maid that he was a gentleman. It was the finest fortress in the land.

As much as he was caught up with his new life, he did not forget the old one and he had a strong sense of duty to those he had spent the best part of his life with, not least of whom was Lénaïg. He wanted to pay her a personal visit and explain that, despite his betrothal, he still cared for her and their son and would make provision for them. He wanted Anthony to shadow Tom as his reeve, and eventually take over that post when Tom felt it was time to retire.

His visit to Threlkeld was not without some trepidation, but he did not expect the furious reaction he got from Lénaïg. She took the news badly, first of all weeping scalding tears and then cold anger, threatening that he would never see Anthony again.

"What did I do wrong, Mother?" he pleaded of Bess. "I told her I would take care of her and acknowledge my son. What did she expect? Did she think the King would give me permission to marry her?"

"You men are insensitive beasts," scolded Bess. "Why did you not consult me about this matter first? It needs a woman's touch, and you may be a Lord but you are a still a blundering fool."

"Insensitive? She is the one threatening to take my son from me," blustered Henry. "She can't do that, I can force her to surrender him to my care."

"Do that and his mind will be turned against you for good," replied Bess sharply. "You have done enough damage already. Of all the women at the King's court, you had to pick the only one she knows. How do you think she feels? Before this, she had a future. She had hope. All she sees before her now is despair and sorrow."

"What would you have me do, Mother?" pleaded Henry. "I meant no harm to anyone."

"Go now from this place, and leave her to nurse her wounds. I will talk with her. You go and pay your respects at Yanwath Hall and I will call for you when the time is right."

Tom led a reluctant Henry away. Henry shook his head, bewildered now, the gloss of his newfound elevation painfully peeled away.

"Why did she take the news so badly, Fatha? She talks like she hates me, yet I still care for her."

"Jealousy and love are sisters, son," explained Tom sagely. "Yon lass is hurt and she sees thee departing from your old life together. You are her tether stake. She's bound to feel a sense of loss, it's only natural. I don't envy thee. There's more to being a great Lord than meets the eye."

Two days later, Bess called for Henry and there, waiting for him at Threlkeld Hall, was Lénaïg, with their son, Anthony.

She rushed into his arms and clung on to him for dear life, weeping and heaving, her heart churning up great sobs of emotion. She smothered him with tear-dewed kisses, holding his face in her hands. Over her shoulder he saw young Anthony blinking back at him. He felt embarrassed, like he should not be holding Lénaïg now that he was betrothed. For once in his life he did not know how to react, and looked to Bess for guidance.

"You do not know the ways of the nobility, my son, and you do not know the ways of the world," said Bess in a rueful, pitying manner.

"You will not be sharing the same bed chamber at Skipton Castle with Lady Anne. She will have her own room. You will sleep in your own bed with your trusted servants sleeping on the floor. The King has given his cousin to you as a breeding mare so that he might form a strong alliance with the north. Couple with her and produce sons. That is all that is expected of you. She will be your wife and you may profess to one and all that you love her dearly, but there is one here that will always love you more. You must make a choice. Leave and take her with you, and you will also leave with your son."

Henry made to object but Bess stayed him with her hand.

"There are many manors in the lordship of Skipton. No one will raise an eye if the mighty Lord Clifford grants one to his mistress. Then you will be able to visit her and see your son grow up. You cannot separate the two. If you try and take him away from her, she will have nothing. You do not have it in you to be so cruel."

Henry hesitated. He looked from Bess to Lénaïg, to Anthony and then to Bess again for inspiration.

"Do what your heart tells you, son," Bess said, nodding in the direction of a desperate and anxious-looking Lénaïg.

To Lénaïg she turned and said, "Men were made for us, and we for them."

Henry acted without thinking; he held Lénaïg and his son in his great arms, kissing them both and trying to blink away his tears.

"Skipton it is then. Let's pick you a fine house," he said, trying to look stern.

Lénaïg clung on to his neck and said, "It is not unto my ear that you speak but into my heart. When you kissed me on the lips, it was not those ruby rose buds but my soul that you touched. I have already told thee, I will not be parted from thee, ever."

All the while Tom looked on, shaking his head and thinking, "This is another fine mess, and I know who will be the one to clean it up."

At Skipton Castle, great preparations were taking place in preparation for the return of the Cliffords, and the marriage feast. The quartered arms with the three stags of the Stanleys were removed and burned and replaced with the ancient arms of the rightful occupant. To provide his bride with suitable apartments, Henry modernized the castle, improving the Great Hall with a new window, and built on to the east curtain wall a two-storey domestic range, its windows opening on to the courtyard. To mark its construction, he put a stone tablet above the door of the new wing with the Clifford and Vipont shields with a Wyvern[28] crest. The arms of St John he placed on the south side of the Conduit Court to welcome his new bride.

New tapestries were hung, which rivalled those Henry had seen at the King's Court. He was particularly pleased with one that depicted the Labours of the Month, showing the peasants about their seasonal tasks. It minded him of his recent occupation.

Lady Anne was not disappointed with her new home and Henry took great pride in showing her around. He had made a comfortable residence for her within the strong, foreboding walls of the castle and was attentive to her every need.

His heart still raced when he saw her of a morning and he could not help but feel guilt about his trysts with Lénaïg. His relationship with Anne was different, though. He almost worshipped her from afar. Her looks, fine

---

28. A dragon with a serpent's tail.

manners and tinkling laughter held him in thrall. He was fascinated by her and impatient for their betrothal and wedding feast.

The prior of Bolton Abbey conducted the marriage ceremony and the banquet was held in the Great Hall with its newly-hung tapestries.

Henry had given equal ranking to his old 'shepherd' family when it came to the seating arrangements, and this caused some raised eyebrows amongst the noble guests, but none dared object as they knew he would take great offence.

Boys, half-naked because of the heat, turned the spit in the great fireplace and the bread ovens were working constantly. The nobles at the top table were served good Burgundy wine, but Ralph and Luke eschewed this with a demand for good English ale.

Tristram Bolling, without any prompting, stood on his feet and proposed a toast to the happy couple.

"My lords, my ladies and gentlemen, good people of Skipton gathered here today to witness this joining of two of the great families of England. Who would have thought it possible, after all the troubles that this noble realm has gone through, that this match might have happened? I'll tell you why this has been made possible. It has been made possible because it has been ordained by none other than God.

"Our heavenly Lord has seen it fit to pluck a shepherd boy from these very hills and make him into a mighty lord, fit to marry the most beautiful bride in all of Christendom."

At this Lady Anne giggled and Henry smiled at her indulgently.

"I feel like Lord Clifford is one of my sons and I am right happy for him on this day," Tristram continued. "May the Good Lord bless this happy couple with many sons and heirs and as much bounty as is their due. Good people, I give you the Shepherd Lord and his bride."

Everyone rose to their feet to give the toast and the kitchen boys stopped their work to witness everyone in such a jolly mood.

Later that week, Henry sought out Tom, who was idly watching a flock of cross-bred sheep on Rombald's Moor.

"I wonder how they'll fare this winter, Fatha?" asked Henry.

Tom stirred from his reverie and looked surprised to see him. "My Lord Henry?"

Henry stopped him with, "Moses, Fatha, I'll always be your Mo, and never want it any other way. I owe you my life and you have been the best fatha that a man could ask for. If I can lead my life as good as thee, I'll be a contented man. I know you are longing to get back to your sheep and I'll buy you your own flock, but I need you and Mother at hand. Families have to stick together. I'd be lost in the wilderness without you."

The two big men embraced and Tom couldn't help but feel the tears pricking his eyes.

"You big daft beggar," he said. "Am I ever to be rid of thee?"

They both laughed and Henry said, "I reckon you'll need a good shepherd come lambing time. Tha's not getting any younger, tha' knows."

Not everyone in the realm was happy though. News of the dramatic restoration of Henry Clifford and the legendary exploits of the Shepherd Lord were widely told. None more so than the sinister tale of Eldroth the assassin, and how he met his fate, suffocated by a fleece at the hands of the Shepherd Lord's protector, Tom Lawkland. History twists in on itself and folds the run of years that touch the present with a cold hand.

Eldroth's bastard son, Angel, sat in a tavern, brooding at the news of the happy couple's nuptials. His life had not been an easy one. Born of an Italian whore, accompanying condottieri in the Yorkist camp, he had little to remember his childhood with any fondness. There was no doubt he was Eldroth's son though, for he bore a striking resemblance to his father. Eldroth had taken a real shine to him as he was a real broth of a boy, always at the centre of trouble with the other brats in the camp. He laughed ironically at his choice of name and said he should have been called Devil's Spawn instead. Angel made up for his lack of stature with an innate cruelty and a capacity to withstand pain. Eldroth took time to teach him wicked ways and how to deceive others. At an early age, he taught him how to be a killer and Angel had no compunction about drowning unwanted babies, plucked, bawling from the camp whores. He took a pleasure in the pain of others. Even his own mother was revolted by him. The only one that had ever cared about him or shown any interest in him was Eldroth. And that man was dead at the hands of the Clifford family, or as good as.

Well, he was not about to let that death go unlamented. Someone would pay. They all would pay. He'd find a way to do it.

But Henry Clifford could not have been happier. He paid many visits to Lady Anne's chamber. The sign for him to enter their marriage bed was when the curtains on the carved oak four-poster bed were partly open. An 'open invitation', and this was the sign for him to get rid of the servants slumbering on the floor and warm himself against the smooth lustrous flesh of his Nut-Brown Maid.

Thus, it was no surprise to anyone that, nine months later, she bore him a son. Another Henry. A strong, lusty boy. Amongst the other emotions that most fathers feel at the birth of their first child, Henry had a great feeling of relief. He had sired a son and heir. He had been accepted by the nobility. His wife, Anne, truly loved him. And his other family were nearby, close to hand whenever he needed them.

Above the gatehouse, he had the masons carve the word 'desormais' – henceforth. From this moment on, his life was going to change. It is still there to this day. He raised his newborn son to show him the new inscription. "Look, Henry," he said to the smiling, gurgling infant. "Desormais. Skipton Castle has a new heir. From now on things are different. Our lives will change."

How right he was. But not in the way he thought.

TO BE CONTINUED

IN THE SEQUEL TO
THE SHEPHERD LORD

IN THE SEQUEL, HENRY'S LIFE TAKES ON a dramatic change. Angel's revenge deprives him of one of the strong ties with his old life. His newfound wealth is not to his liking either. He exchanges the rich trappings of Skipton Castle for Barden Tower, a simple hunting lodge where he can escape the pressures of high office and devote his time to studying astronomy and gaining the education he'd missed out on.

His son, Henry, brought up in the ostentation of the King's court, rebels against his father's parsimonious ways and takes matters into his own hands. The young man helps himself to wealth and gets into deep trouble before eventually reconciling himself with his father.

The Shepherd Lord cannot escape the Cliffords' martial roots for long, though, and he takes up a chief command at the Battle of Flodden where James IV of Scotland is killed and he brings many captured Scottish cannon back to the castle.

Tom Lawkland is still there throughout, to guide him through his darkest hours and see his charge take on the honours he justly deserves.

HISTORICAL NOTE

Many of the characters in this book existed. Some are my invention but only in the sense that characters like them must have existed for the Shepherd Lord to lead such a life.

Henry Clifford's life is well documented, apart from the period 1461–1485 when he was in hiding. We do know that whilst he was in hiding at Londesborough, his mother felt sufficiently worried about his safety to move him yet again to Westmorland, under the watchful eye of Sir Lancelot Threlkeld, whom she later married, as she does in the book.

Henry did have a natural-born son named Anthony. So, if he had a son, Henry must have had a lover whilst he was in hiding. That's why I conjured up Lénaïg.

As I've said, Henry's whereabouts were a closely-guarded secret, but parties loyal to the House of York wanted to hunt him down. His father, John 'Blackface' Clifford, or the 'Butcher' as he was known, was famous enough to figure largely in Shakespeare's Henry VI. He is said to have killed the Dukes of York and Arundel and this would have been enough to warrant the manhunt for his son. This gave me free rein to come up with Dickon Hoccleve, Edward Lambert and of course the malevolent Eldroth.

Lord William Stanley's fickle and shambling nature are well known in history books and he did occupy Skipton Castle after the Cliffords were attainted but in later years it passed into the custody of Richard III, before it was restored to its rightful owner, Henry. Its walls never were breached. Even Oliver Cromwell could not take the castle by force during the English Civil War when it was a Royalist stronghold. He had to negotiate honourable terms with its redoubtable occupant, another Anne Clifford, before its surrender.

Tristram Bolling's father, Robert, was called upon by John Clifford, Commander of the Northern Musters, under Henry VI "to repair forthwith, and not fail at their peril, to join His Majestie's forces at Doncaster," in prepa-

147

ration for the Battle of Towton. After the Lancastrian forces were routed, he escaped from the field of battle but lost his lands. It took him fourteen years to get them back, thanks to a helping hand from Richard III (he was still Duke of Gloucester then) who put in a good word with his big brother, Edward IV. I am not entirely sure he took part in the cavalry charge from Castle Hill Wood, but his son Tristram was definitely with him and the Battle of Towton must have figured heavily in his mind for the rest of his days, for in his will it says:

"I bequeath in honour of my mortuary my best horse wt. sadyll and bridyll, jake, salet, bowe and harnes, sword and buckler as I went to the war."

Since I wrote the novel, new research suggests that Tristram was a member of The Flower of Craven that took part in the assault at Ferrybridge as one of John Clifford's mounted archers. If this is true, this places him as a survivor of two bloody massacres in as many days. In the book I have him playing an important role at the beginning and then again making a big show at the end. There is no historical reference to him helping restore Henry Clifford to his lands but he's a relative; it's my book, and I can, so I did.

I have to put a word in for Richard III, a character much maligned by Shakespeare and condemned to history as a crook-backed scoundrel. The serious historians know differently, and Richard was a good, fair-minded King and showed the Northern Earls great favour. Yorkshiremen still flock to his cause after all these years.

Now we come to the Nut-Brown Maid, Anne St John, cousin to Henry VII. Legend has the young Shepherd Lord encountering her, lost on the fells, and taking her back to his home. The poem, *The Nut Brown Maid*, alludes to her happening upon the outlawed Henry, and I was really intrigued by this. I was even more fixated when I discovered that the poem was all but lost for posterity. It was Samuel Pepys who found it amongst a bundle of accounts in Antwerp, of all places. Mysteriously, I had to find my copy in an antiquarian bookshop in Brisbane, so after this communion with the past, you can perhaps understand why I think this story must be told before it is lost to obscurity again. Despite all the intrigue surrounding this story, Henry Clifford did get to marry his Nut-Brown Maid, and they had a son and heir, another Henry, who became Earl of Cumberland.

Finally, I have to confess to making up the novel's central character, Tom Lawkland. There is no recorded entry of such a person, but it was said that Henry was given to be raised by his wet nurse, who was married to a shepherd. What struck me was the parallels with Joseph, the father of Jesus. Someone must have nurtured and protected young Henry but no one makes mention of it in any book that I know, just like very little is said of Joseph in the bible. It set me thinking about such a man, a man of strong character. Like the infant Jesus, Henry was hunted down by evil men. Like Joseph, Tom Lawkland had to raise someone else's son at great danger to himself. It must have taken a strong man to do this. Someone who didn't make a big fuss about it and just got on with the job.

So, was there really a Shepherd Lord? No one can say for sure whether Henry Clifford really was a shepherd, but I ask you this. How many York-shiremen do you know would let a young lad stand idly by whilst there was work to be done?

I'll bet Henry made a damn fine shepherd.

THE SHEPHERD LORD'S DOMAIN

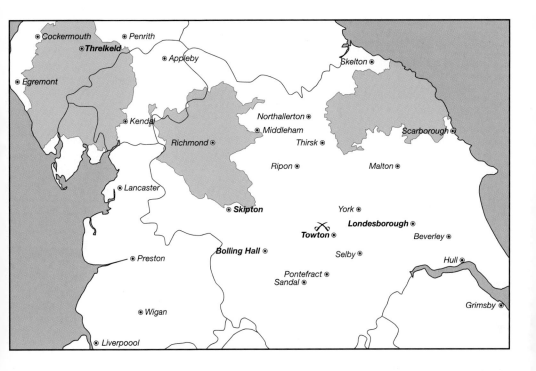

Skipton Castle is open to the public and is one of the finest examples of a medieval castle in Britain.

www.skiptoncastle.co.uk

Bolling Hall is now a museum and is described as 'the jewel in Bradford's crown.'
www.bradfordmuseums.org/bollinghall/index.htm

Towton has a guided tour every Palm Sunday on the anniversary of the battle.
www.towton.org.uk/

JOHN LORD CLIFFORD
BLACK FACED CLIFFORD
KILLED AT BATTLE OF TOWTON
1461

Thought to be the first portrait of a Clifford. Lord John 'Blackface' Clifford. 9th Lord of Skipton and father of the Shepherd Lord. This painting is of sixteenth century origin, hence the ruff.

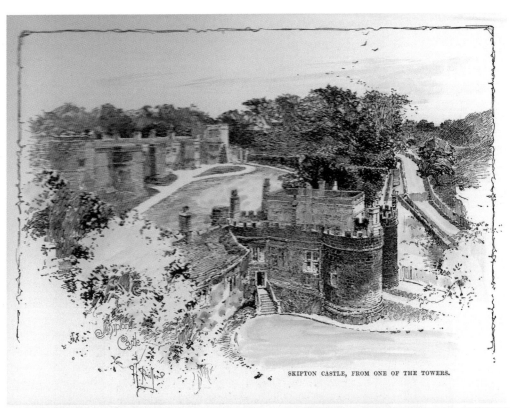

SKIPTON CASTLE, FROM ONE OF THE TOWERS.

BOLLING OLD HALL. BRADFORD.

D.F & C York

Top: *Skipton Castle from a print dated 1892.*

Bottom: *Bolling Hall. The left wing of the building is the original Pele Tower built by the Bolling family.*

Henry VI from an engraving dated 1803. It is said that Tristram Bolling was fond of old King Henry and kept a portrait of him at Bolling Hall.

154

Bibliography

The History Of Skipton. W. Harbutt Dawson (1832).

Song at the Feast of Brougham Castle. William Wordsworth (1807).

The Nut-Brown Maid. Anon. Printed in Antwerp (1502).

Blood Red Roses. Andrew Boardman, Andrea Burgess, Jennifer Coughlan, Helen Cox, Hugh Griffiths, Malin Holst, Shannon Novak, Graeme Rimer, Thom Richardson, Tim Sutherland and John Waller. Revised edition published 2007.

The Shepherd Lord of Skipton Castle. Richard T. Spence (1994).

Sir William Stanley of Holt. Jean M. Gidman (2003).

The Idiomatic Tour of Skipton Castle. Don Howard and Keith Stephenson (2003).

Lancaster against York. Trevor Royle (2008).

Medieval Lives. Terry Jones and Alan Ereira (2005).

Who Murdered Chaucer – A Medieval Mystery. Terry Jones, Terry Dolan, Juliette Dor, Alan Fletcher, Robert Yeager (2006).

The Time Traveller's Guide to Medieval England. Ian Mortimer (2008).

Bolling Family History – Eight Centuries of Growth. Major-General Alexander R. Bolling Jr (2004).

The Histories of Bolton and Bowling. William Cudworth (1891).

Henry VI. William Shakespeare.

Blood and Roses – Letters from the Paston Family. Helen Castor (2004).

With special thanks to the Battle of Towton Society, Members of Richard III Foundation for their suggestions on other research material, and Bradford's Bolling Hall Museum Staff.

A Song at the Feast of Brougham Castle

UPON THE RESTORATION OF LORD CLIFFORD, THE
SHEPHERD, TO THE ESTATES AND HONOURS OF HIS
ANCESTORS

HIGH in the breathless Hall the Minstrel sate,
And Emont's murmur mingled with the Song.
The words of ancient time I thus translate,
A festal strain that hath been silent long:
"From town to town, from tower to tower,
The red rose is a gladsome flower.
Her thirty years of winter past,
The red rose is revived at last;
She lifts her head for endless spring,
For everlasting blossoming:
Both roses flourish, red and white:
In love and sisterly delight
The two that were at strife are blended,
And all old troubles now are ended.
Joy! joy to both! but most to her
Who is the flower of Lancaster!
Behold her how She smiles to-day
On this great throng, this bright array!
Fair greeting doth she send to all

157

From every corner of the hall;
But chiefly from above the board
Where sits in state our rightful Lord,
A Clifford to his own restored!
They came with banner, spear, and shield,
And it was proved in Bosworth-field.
Not long the Avenger was withstood--
Earth helped him with the cry of blood:
St. George was for us, and the might
Of blessed Angels crowned the right.
Loud voice the Land has uttered forth,
We loudest in the faithful north:
Our fields rejoice, our mountains ring,
Our streams proclaim a welcoming;
Our strong-abodes and castles see
The glory of their loyalty.
How glad is Skipton at this hour--
Though lonely, a deserted Tower;
Knight, squire, and yeoman, page and groom:
We have them at the feast of Brough'm.
How glad Pendragon--though the sleep
Of years be on her!--She shall reap
A taste of this great pleasure, viewing
As in a dream her own renewing.
Rejoiced is Brough, right glad I deem
Beside her little humble stream;
And she that keepeth watch and ward
Her statelier Eden's course to guard;
They both are happy at this hour,
Though each is but a lonely Tower:--
But here is perfect joy and pride
For one fair House by Emont's side,
This day, distinguished without peer
To see her Master and to cheer--
Him, and his Lady-mother dear!

Oh! it was a time forlorn
When the fatherless was born--
Give her wings that she may fly,
Or she sees her infant die!
Swords that are with slaughter wild
Hunt the Mother and the Child.
Who will take them from the light?
--Yonder is a man in sight--
Yonder is a house--but where?
No, they must not enter there.
To the caves, and to the brooks,
To the clouds of heaven she looks;
She is speechless, but her eyes
Pray in ghostly agonies.
Blissful Mary, Mother mild,
Maid and Mother undefiled,
Save a Mother and her Child!
Now Who is he that bounds with joy
On Carrock's side, a Shepherd-boy?
No thoughts hath he but thoughts that pass
Light as the wind along the grass.
Can this be He who hither came
In secret, like a smothered flame?
O'er whom such thankful tears were shed
For shelter, and a poor man's bread!
God loves the Child; and God hath willed
That those dear words should be fulfilled,
The Lady's words, when forced away,
The last she to her Babe did say:
'My own, my own, thy Fellow-guest
I may not be; but rest thee, rest,
For lowly shepherd's life is best!'
Alas! when evil men are strong
No life is good, no pleasure long.
The Boy must part from Mosedale's groves,

And leave Blencathara's rugged coves,
And quit the flowers that summer brings
To Glenderamakin's lofty springs;
Must vanish, and his careless cheer
Be turned to heaviness and fear.
--Give Sir Lancelot Threlkeld praise!
Hear it, good man, old in days!
Thou tree of covert and of rest
For this young Bird that is distrest;
Among thy branches safe he lay,
And he was free to sport and play,
When falcons were abroad for prey.
A recreant harp, that sings of fear
And heaviness in Clifford's ear!
I said, when evil men are strong,
No life is good, no pleasure long,
A weak and cowardly untruth!
Our Clifford was a happy Youth,
And thankful through a weary time,
That brought him up to manhood's prime.
--Again he wanders forth at will,
And tends a flock from hill to hill:
His garb is humble; ne'er was seen
Such garb with such a noble mien;
Among the shepherd grooms no mate
Hath he, a Child of strength and state!
Yet lacks not friends for simple glee,
Nor yet for higher sympathy.
To his side the fallow-deer
Came, and rested without fear;
The eagle, lord of land and sea,
Stooped down to pay him fealty;
And both the undying fish that swim
Through Bowscale-tarn did wait on him;
The pair were servants of his eye

In their immortality;
And glancing, gleaming, dark or bright,
Moved to and fro, for his delight.
He knew the rocks which Angels haunt
Upon the mountains visitant;
He hath kenned them taking wing:
And into caves where Faeries sing
He hath entered; and been told
By Voices how men lived of old.
Among the heavens his eye can see
The face of thing that is to be;
And, if that men report him right,
His tongue could whisper words of might.
--Now another day is come,
Fitter hope, and nobler doom;
He hath thrown aside his crook,
And hath buried deep his book;
Armour rusting in his halls
On the blood of Clifford calls;--
'Quell the Scot,' exclaims the Lance--
Bear me to the heart of France,
Is the longing of the Shield--
Tell thy name, thou trembling Field;
Field of death, where'er thou be,
Groan thou with our victory!
Happy day, and mighty hour,
When our Shepherd, in his power,
Mailed and horsed, with lance and sword,
To his ancestors restored
Like a re-appearing Star,
Like a glory from afar,
First shall head the flock of war!"

THE SHEPHERD LORD

Alas! the impassioned minstrel did not know
How, by Heaven's grace, this Clifford's heart was framed,
How he, long forced in humble walks to go,
Was softened into feeling, soothed, and tamed.

Love had he found in huts where poor men lie;
His daily teachers had been woods and rills,
The silence that is in the starry sky,
The sleep that is among the lonely hills.

In him the savage virtue of the Race,
Revenge, and all ferocious thoughts were dead:
Nor did he change; but kept in lofty place
The wisdom which adversity had bred.

Glad were the vales, and every cottage hearth;
The Shepherd-Lord was honoured more and more;
And, ages after he was laid in earth,
"The good Lord Clifford" was the name he bore.
1807.

THE NUT-BROWN MAID

He: BE it right or wrong, these men among
On women do complain;
Affirming this, how that it is
A labour spent in vain
To love them wele; for never a dele
They love a man again:
For let a man do what he can
Their favour to attain,
Yet if a new to them pursue,
Their first true lover than
Laboureth for naught; for from her thought
He is a banished man.

She: I say not nay, but that all day
It is both written and said
That woman's faith is, as who saith,
All utterly decayd:
But nevertheless, right good witnèss
In this case might be laid
That they love true and continue:
Record the Nut-brown Maid,
Which, when her love came her to prove,
To her to make his moan,
Would not depart; for in her heart
She loved but him alone.

THE SHEPHERD LORD

He: Then between us let us discuss
What was all the manere
Between them two: we will also
Tell all the pain in fere
That she was in. Now I begin,
So that ye me answere:
Wherefore all ye that present be,
I pray you, give an ear.
I am the Knight. I come by night,
As secret as I can,
Saying, Alas! thus standeth the case,
I am a banished man.

She: And I your will for to fulfil
In this will not refuse;
Trusting to show, in wordes few,
That men have an ill use –
To their own shame – women to blame,
And causeless them accuse.
Therefore to you I answer now,
All women to excuse –
Mine own heart dear, with you what cheer?
I pray you, tell anone;
For, in my mind, of all mankind
I love but you alone.

He: It standeth so: a deed is do
Whereof great harm shall grow:
My destiny is for to die
A shameful death, I trow;
Or else to flee. The t' one must be.
None other way I know
But to withdraw as an outlàw,
And take me to my bow.
Wherefore adieu, mine own heart true!

None other rede I can:
For I must to the green-wood go,
Alone, a banished man.

She: O Lord, what is this worldis bliss,
That changeth as the moon!
My summer's day in lusty May
Is darked before the noon.
I hear you say, farewell: Nay, nay,
We dèpart not so soon.
Why say ye so? whither will ye go?
Alas! what have ye done?
All my welfàre to sorrow and care
Should change, if ye were gone:
For, in my mind, of all mankind
I love but you alone.

He: I can believe it shall you grieve,
And somewhat you distrain;
But afterward, your paines hard
Within a day or twain
Shall soon aslake; and ye shall take
Comfort to you again.
Why should ye ought? for, to make thought,
Your labour were in vain.
And thus I do; and pray you to,
As hartely as I can:
For I must to the green-wood go,
Alone, a banished man.

She: Now, sith that ye have showed to me
The secret of your mind,
I shall be plain to you again,
Like as ye shall me find.
Sith it is so that ye will go,

I will not live behind.
Shall never be said the Nut-brown Maid
Was to her love unkind.
Make you ready, for so am I,
Although it were anone:
For, in my mind, of all mankind
I love but you alone.

He: Yet I you rede to take good heed
What men will think and say:
Of young, of old, it shall be told
That ye be gone away
Your wanton will for to fulfil,
In green-wood you to play;
And that ye might for your delight
No longer make delay
Rather than ye should thus for me
Be called an ill womàn
Yet would I to the green-wood go,
Alone, a banished man.

She: Though it be sung of old and young
That I should be to blame,
Theirs be the charge that speak so large
In hurting of my name:
For I will prove that faithful love
It is devoid of shame;
In your distress and heaviness
To part with you the same:
And sure all tho that do not so
True lovers are they none:
For in my mind, of all mankind
I love but you alone.

He: I counsel you, Remember how
It is no maiden's law
Nothing to doubt, but to run out
To wood with an outlàw.
For ye must there in your hand bear
A bow ready to draw;
And as a thief thus must you live
Ever in dread and awe;
Whereby to you great harm might grow:
Yet had I liever than
That I had to the green-wood go,
Alone, a banished man.

She: I think not nay but as ye say;
It is no maiden's lore;
But love may make me for your sake,
As I have said before,
To come on foot, to hunt and shoot,
To get us meat and store;
For so that I your company
May have, I ask no more.
From which to part it maketh my heart
As cold as any stone;
For, in my mind, of all mankind
I love but you alone.

He: For an outlàw this is the law,
That men him take and bind:
Without pitie, hangèd to be,
And waver with the wind.
If I had need (as God forbede!)
What socours could ye find?
Forsooth I trow, you and your bow
For fear would draw behind.
And no mervail; for little avail

167

Were in your counsel than:
Wherefore I'll to the green-wood go,
Alone, a banished man.

She: Right well know ye that women be
But feeble for to fight;
No womanhede it is, indeed,
To be bold as a knight:
Yet in such fear if that ye were
With enemies day and night,
I would withstand, with bow in hand,
To grieve them as I might,
And you to save; as women have
From death men many one:
For, in my mind, of all mankind
I love but you alone.

He: Yet take good hede; for ever I drede
That ye could not sustain
The thorny ways, the deep vallèys,
The snow, the frost, the rain,
The cold, the heat; for dry or wete,
We must lodge on the plain;
And, us above, no other roof
But a brake bush or twain:
Which soon should grieve you, I believe;
And ye would gladly than
That I had to the green-wood go,
Alone, a banished man.

She: Sith I have here been partynere
With you of joy and bliss,
I must alsò part of your woe
Endure, as reason is:
Yet I am sure of one pleasùre,

And shortly it is this —
That where ye be, me seemeth, pardé,
I could not fare amiss.
Without more speech I you beseech
That we were shortly gone;
For, in my mind, of all mankind
I love but you alone.

He: If ye go thyder, ye must consider,
When ye have lust to dine,
There shall no meat be for to gete,
Nether bere, ale, ne wine,
Ne shetès clean, to lie between,
Made of thread and twine;
None other house, but leaves and boughs,
To cover your head and mine.
Lo, mine heart sweet, this ill diète
Should make you pale and wan:
Wherefore I'll to the green-wood go,
Alone, a banished man.

She: Among the wild deer such an archère,
As men say that ye be,
Ne may not fail of good vitayle
Where is so great plentè:
And water clear of the rivere
Shall be full sweet to me;
With which in hele I shall right wele
Endure, as ye shall see;
And, or we go, a bed or two
I can provide anone;
For, in my mind, of all mankind
I love but you alone.

He: Lo yet, before, ye must do more,
If ye will go with me:
As, cut your hair up by your ear,
Your kirtle by the knee;
With bow in hand for to withstand
Your enemies, if need be:
And this same night, before daylight,
To woodward will I flee.
If that ye will all this fulfil,
Do it shortly as ye can:
Else will I to the green-wood go,
Alone, a banished man.

She: I shall as now do more for you
Than 'longeth to womanhede;
To short my hair, a bow to bear,
To shoot in time of need.
O my sweet mother! before all other
For you I have most drede!
But now, adieu! I must ensue
Where fortune doth me lead.
All this make ye: Now let us flee;
The day cometh fast upon:
For, in my mind, of all mankind
I love but you alone.

He: Nay, nay, not so; ye shall not go,
And I shall tell you why —
Your appetite is to be light
Of love, I well espy:
For, right as ye have said to me,
In likewise hardily
Ye would answere whosoever it were,
In way of company:
It is said of old, Soon hot, soon cold;

And so is a womàn:
Wherefore I to the wood will go,
Alone, a banished man.

She: If ye take heed, it is no need
Such words to say to me;
For oft ye prayed, and long assayed,
Or I loved you, pardè:
And though that I of ancestry
A baron's daughter be,
Yet have you proved how I you loved,
A squire of low degree;
And ever shall, whatso befall
To die therefore anone;
For, in my mind, of all mankind
I love but you alone.

He: A baron's child to be beguiled,
It were a cursèd deed!
To be felàw with an outlaw —
Almighty God forbede!
Yet better were the poor squyere
Alone to forest yede
Than ye shall say another day
That by my cursèd rede
Ye were betrayed. Wherefore, good maid,
The best rede that I can,
Is, that I to the green-wood go,
Alone, a banished man.

She: Whatever befall, I never shall
Of this thing be upbraid:
But if ye go, and leave me so,
Then have ye me betrayed.
Remember you wele, how that ye dele;

171

For if ye, as ye said,
Be so unkind to leave behind
Your love, the Nut-brown Maid,
Trust me truly that I shall die
Soon after ye be gone:
For, in my mind, of all mankind
I love but you alone.

He: If that ye went, ye should repent;
For in the forest now
I have purveyed me of a maid
Whom I love more than you:
Another more fair than ever ye were
I dare it well avow;
And of you both each should be wroth
With other, as I trow:
It were mine ease to live in peace;
So will I, if I can:
Wherefore I to the wood will go,
Alone, a banished man.

She: Though in the wood I understood
Ye had a paramour,
All this may nought remove my thought,
But that I will be your:
And she shall find me soft and kind
And courteis every hour;
Glad to fulfil all that she will
Command me, to my power:
For had ye, lo, an hundred mo,
Yet would I be that one:
For, in my mind, of all mankind
I love but you alone.

He: Mine own dear love, I see the prove
That ye be kind and true;
Of maid, of wife, in all my life,
The best that ever I knew.
Be merry and glad; be no more sad;
The case is changèd new;
For it were ruth that for your truth
Ye should have cause to rue.
Be not dismayed, whatsoever I said
To you when I began:
I will not to the green-wood go;
I am no banished man.

She: These tidings be more glad to me
Than to be made a queen,
If I were sure they should endure;
But it is often seen
When men will break promise they speak
The wordis on the splene.
Ye shape some wile me to beguile,
And steal from me, I ween:
Then were the case worse than it was,
And I more woebegone:
For, in my mind, of all mankind
I love but you alone.

He: Ye shall not nede further to drede:
I will not disparàge
You (God defend), sith you descend
Of so great a linàge.
Now understand: to Westmoreland,
Which is my heritage,
I will you bring; and with a ring,
By way of marriàge
I will you take, and lady make,

As shortly as I can:
Thus have you won an Earles son,
And not a banished man.

Here may ye see that women be
In love meek, kind, and stable;
Let never man reprove them than,
Or call them variable;
But rather pray God that we may
To them be comfortable;
Which sometime proveth such as He loveth,
If they be charitable.
For sith men would that women should
Be meek to them each one;
Much more ought they to God obey,
And serve but Him alone.

GLOSSARY

never a dele – never a bit.
Than – then.
in fere – in company together.
rede I can – counsel I know.
part with – share with.
Tho – those.
Hele – health.
Yede – went.
on the spleen – that is, in haste.